DOWNWARD DEATH

STELLA BIXBY

FERRY TAIL PUBLISHING LLC

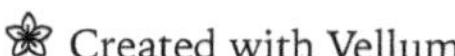 Created with Vellum

For my Family

The letter arrived the moment I was leaving.

I'd only lived with my boyfriend a couple months, but in the middle of an argument, I let my guard down, and he freaked—my cue to run. Or rather, move on.

I had two key life skills—speed packing all of my worldly possessions and eating gobs of chocolate chip cookies. So, when I decided to go, all my stuff was in Big Bertha—my massive suitcase—before I could change my mind.

Not that I would have.

I never did.

Life wasn't meant to be lived in the rearview mirror.

Once people caught a glimpse of who I really was, they never looked at me the same. I'd gone through more friends, boyfriends, and foster families than I could count. Perhaps that was the reason my mom left me at a fire station when I was an infant.

Either way, it didn't matter. I had a great life.

Penelope—my tiny pet pig—and I did fine on our own. I actually preferred living in my retro Volkswagen Microbus, Mona, to living with a boyfriend. She was cozy, if a little temperamental, but she had absolutely zero expectations or judgment.

I hoisted Big Bertha into Mona's side door, careful not to hit the brand-new equipment I'd recently spent every last dime on to start my business—a traveling mind, body, and soul health club for those of advanced age. I'd gotten my bachelor's degree in therapeutic recreation, intending to work for a hospital, but after a year and a half, I hadn't been able to find a job. So, I transitioned my traveling home into a traveling home office. I'd only just painted the words Relief with Ellie on the side.

"Wait." A woman who lived next door in the apartment complex came rushing toward me. I'd never learned her name, but we'd always exchanged friendly smiles and an occasional hello when we crossed paths. "The mailman dropped this in my slot by accident."

She held a large envelope that looked like it had seen better days.

I stared at the package, unable to move.

"You *are* Ellie Vanderwick, right?" she asked.

I'd never gotten mail before. Not mail like this—mail that looked like it came from a relative or friend.

"Do you want it or . . ."

I closed my mouth and reached out a hand. "Thanks."

"No problem." She hesitated. "I love what you've done with your hair. I could never get away with such bold color, but on you, it looks amazing. He'll be sorry he let you go."

I ran a hand through my hair. It had pulled itself into tight curls. And if I could guess, it was probably streaked with red from the argument. I took a breath, held it a few seconds, and let it out. My curls relaxed. If I could get my heart rate under control, the color would go back to its normal white.

"Oh," she said. "Thanks again for bringing Zoomy back the other day. I don't know how she got by me."

Zoomy was her dog and Penelope's best friend. They loved to play when we were out on walks or potty breaks. When I found Zoomy out by our usual potty break location without her person, it was only right to take her back. Anyone would have done the same.

"It's no problem," I said. "Penelope will miss playing with Zoomy."

"You'll have to come back by for a playdate sometime," she said with a smile. Then turned and walked away.

I almost forgot about the envelope in my hand.

Almost.

The return address—handwritten in a beautiful script —was from Cliff Haven, Iowa. It looked like it had been forwarded a half-dozen times. The postmark was March, nearly six months ago.

What stunned me most, though, was the name above the return address.

Esme Vanderwick.

I'd never met another Vanderwick. My records stated when my mother dropped me off at the fire station, she'd left a note with my name and a few hundred dollars for whoever took me in.

I'd searched sporadically for another Vanderwick, but

I'd always come up empty-handed. Apparently, I only had to go a couple states east.

I turned the envelope over and hesitated. The bright Colorado sun warmed my bare shoulders, but goosebumps overtook my arms.

My entire life, I'd been curious about my family—my real family. But with potential answers within my grasp, I wasn't sure how to react. What if it wasn't what I expected? Or hoped for? What if my mother was in jail or something?

Penelope let out an oink from Mona's passenger seat.

She was right. I needed to open this when I wasn't standing out in the open for the world to see.

My scalp tingled in agreement.

I jumped in Mona's side door, slid it closed behind me, and climbed up into the driver's seat next to Penelope.

"What do you think it is?" I asked.

She nudged it with her wiggly little snout.

"Okay, I'll open it."

I didn't dare glance in the mirror to see how my hair was changing. Sometimes it was a blessing. Especially when it warned me of danger. But most of the time, it was just another thing I had to hide. I'd have a heck of a lot more space in my van if I didn't have to store all the hats, scarves, and scrunchies I used to disguise my secret.

I ripped through the envelope where a hole had already started from all the handling it had received. A faint smell of lilac drifted to my nose as I pulled out a stack of documents.

On top was a letter.

To my dearest Ellie,

The time has come for me to pass along what is rightfully yours. Though I hoped we'd be able to meet in the flesh, I don't believe that will come to pass as my life is quickly expiring. At one point in my life, I thought I'd pass my belongings on to my daughter—your mother. But I've decided everything I own is yours and yours alone for you to do with it as you wish. I only hope you'll forgive me for not finding you sooner.

I believe you'll like Cliff Haven. It's a quiet town with hardly any crime and some of the best people I've ever met. Please give it a chance.

Know, my sweet granddaughter, I've loved you with all my heart from the moment I knew you existed.

Esme

Tears pricked at the corners of my eyes. Penelope oinked quietly letting me know my hair had fallen into a slight wave, draping over my shoulders.

I had a grandmother.

I typed Cliff Haven, Iowa into my GPS and turned the key in the ignition. "Penelope, we're going to Iowa."

2

I t took two days to reach Cliff Haven. Mona wasn't keen on going much faster than sixty miles per hour, so we took more back roads than interstate. The last back road led to a cute pink mailbox that matched the address from the envelope.

Tall cornstalks lined either side of a long gravel driveway that deposited a fresh coat of dust onto Mona's pink paint job and made Penelope sneeze. A white house that looked like it had seen better days stood at the end of the drive with a huge red barn off to one side.

"Looks like we're here," I said to Penelope. "Should we go inside?"

Penelope oinked happily.

I pulled a key ring from the envelope, tucking the rest of it under my arm for safe-keeping. Esme said there wasn't much crime, but if someone stole the documents, I'd never be able to prove Esme left all of this to me.

My chest compressed with joy. The closest I'd ever had to a real home was Mona. And though she was the best home I could have ever imagined, standing in front of a real, true house—one that belonged to someone whose blood trickled through my veins—was a feeling I didn't know I'd ever have.

Penelope wiggled her way up the rickety steps to the front door and looked back at me expectantly.

"I'm coming," I said.

I let out a sigh of relief when the key turned in the lock. There was some part of me that thought this was one big, mean prank. Until I opened the door.

A frosty breeze replaced the hot sticky air from outside, and the scent of lilacs tickled my nose. I flipped on a light, illuminating the most beautiful house I'd ever seen.

I took one step in, then another, then another. The dark brick floors contrasted the white plank walls. A long hall connected the front of the house to the back. To the left was a living space, completely furnished with a large fireplace on one wall. An opening on the right led to a small dining room. Paralleling the hall in front of me was a grand wooden staircase with a curved wood banister that shone as if it had just been polished.

"Where do we begin?"

Penelope grunted, then trotted toward the back door.

At the end of the hall, Penelope took a right into a large kitchen complete with a giant farmhouse sink and concrete countertops. For how rickety the house was on the outside, it sure was updated on the inside.

Penelope nosed her way to the refrigerator. "Smart girl. You're hungry, aren't you?"

My stomach growled.

The refrigerator was completely empty besides a half-gallon of milk, a loaf of bread, and a jar of peanut butter. I picked up the milk to find an expiration date a week out. If Esme had died as she said in the letter, why would there be fresh food in the refrigerator?

Panic welled inside me. What if she was still alive, and I'd barged into her house?

"Maybe we should go back outside and ring the bell," I said to Penelope, who looked thoroughly confused at my shutting the refrigerator door. She squealed in protest.

"Shhhh," I said. But it was too late.

"Who are you?" A deep voice said.

I turned to find a man around my age, wearing only a white towel around his waist. His scowl transformed into a broad smile.

My scalp felt like it was on fire. It had taken the better part of the drive to get my hair to settle down. I wasn't about to let my embarrassment ruin that. I took a deep breath. I couldn't give myself away. If I did, they'd run me out of town before I could learn anything about my family.

"I'm Ellie Vanderwick," I said, holding out a hand, trying to keep my eyes off his washboard abs.

He switched hands holding the towel—careful not to let anything show—and shook mine. "I'm Ty." His smile could have been on the cover of a magazine. "I didn't think you'd make it."

"Should I—" I motioned toward the front door.

"No, no. Stay," he said. "I've just been looking after the place since Esme passed. I'm sorry you couldn't meet her."

"Me too," I said. "I only got the letter two days ago. Otherwise, I would have been here sooner."

"It wouldn't have mattered." Ty shifted his weight from one foot to the other. "Esme died the day after she sent it. It was like once she found you, she could finally let go."

I silently wished she wouldn't have.

"How did she die?" I managed, trying to keep my emotions in check.

"Old age, I guess." He shrugged. "You look just like her, you know?"

"How so?" Though the house was furnished, there were no photographs on any of the walls.

"Same eyes, same smile, same hair." His gaze shifted from my eyes to my hair and back again. "Do you bleach it?"

"Nope," I said, relieved I'd been able to keep it in check. "It's always been this way." Well, almost always. But I wouldn't divulge my deepest secrets to a man I'd only just met—a man who was still standing in front of me half-naked.

"Esme's was white too. I thought it was just because she was older, you know?"

"Did you know her well?" I asked.

"She was practically a grandmother to me. I helped when she needed it," he said. "Fixing things, harvesting the corn, normal stuff."

"That's nice of you." I hesitated before I asked my next question. "Did you know her daughter?"

"Your mom?" he asked.

I waited, trying to keep my composure, while excitement and dread built in my chest.

"No." He shook his head, and my chest deflated. "She left when I was a baby."

"And she never came back?"

He shook his head again. "I'm sorry, that's probably not the answer you were looking for."

I brushed off the disappointment and smiled. "It's okay." It was no use getting worked up about something I'd known—or rather, not known—my entire life.

He glanced down, and his face flushed as if at that precise moment he realized he was standing half-naked in the kitchen with a woman he'd just met. "How about I put on some clothes and get out of your hair?"

At the mention of hair, I reached up and touched the messy bun I'd piled on top of my head.

"And help yourself to anything in the fridge," he said. "There's not much, but whatever's there is yours."

"Penelope?" I glanced back into the kitchen after hearing his footsteps on the stairs. But she was nowhere to be seen. "Do you want some food?"

At the mention of food, her head popped out from behind the kitchen island.

"That's what I thought."

***

Ty came back downstairs no more than ten minutes later, carrying a large duffle bag and a backpack. Oh, and he was completely clothed.

"I'll head out. It was nice meeting you. I won't tell

anyone you're here just yet so the town doesn't blow up your fridge with casseroles."

Casseroles would have been a blessing. After the trip's cost, I'd need to look for a job fast if I wanted to eat. "Do you know anywhere in town that's hiring?"

"The café is always looking for waitstaff," Ty said. "If you want, I can put in a good word."

"That would be great. Thank you."

"It's my pleasure." He smiled. "I'll be back to harvest the corn bright and early tomorrow morning."

"Oh, you don't have to," I said. I hadn't ever needed a man's help with my responsibilities. "I'm sure I can handle it."

He scowled briefly. "*You're* going to harvest the corn?"

"Sure." I shrugged. How hard could it be picking some corn? Plus, I could do it fast and get my cardio in. "Do you want a sandwich before you leave?"

"No thanks." Ty grinned. "I'd like our first dinner together to be more special than a peanut butter sandwich."

The burning returned to my scalp.

"Tomorrow, talk to Bex at the café."

"How do I get to the café?" I asked. "I'm not very familiar with the area."

"If you take a left out of the driveway and then a right when you hit pavement, the highway will spit you out in the middle of Cliff Haven. The café is on the left. You can't miss it."

"A left, a right, and it's on the left." I nodded. "I think I can handle that."

"See you around," he said, then walked out the back door.

His pickup truck sounded like a mixture of fireworks and a tank starting up in the garage on the far side of the house. Penelope huddled under a chair.

"Come on now. It's just a truck," I said. "Let's go upstairs." I was giddy to explore the house.

Penelope reluctantly came out from beneath the chair when the sound of Ty's engine could no longer be heard and pranced along next to me.

The upstairs was as grand as the main level. The first doorway led to the room where I assumed Ty had stayed because the antique metal-framed bed was hastily made, and steam still covered the mirror in the attached bathroom.

A dewy bluish-green color adorned the walls, complimenting the tiny embroidered flowers on the silky white bedspread. Two chairs and a table sat in a bay window, and an antique clothing hutch stood next to what looked like a working fireplace.

A small metal stamped sign hung over the main light switch that said Dewdrop. It was the perfect name for the room.

The TV above the fireplace had been left on, and a show about a sexy female tiger superhero concluded with the police thanking the superhero for helping them bag the bad guy.

"Next on nine news at nine." A picture of a cornfield replaced the superhero show credits. "A developer out of Des Moines is looking to cash in on small-town farmland."

A beautiful woman, probably in her mid-fifties and dressed like she'd just come off a New York runway, popped up on the screen. "We're looking to bring beautiful modern housing all across the Midwest, starting right here in the heart of Iowa."

"It's nine o'clock?" I said to Penelope. "That's only eight o'clock Colorado time. Why am I so tired?"

Penelope let out a little grunt. She was tired too.

I switched the TV off and left the room.

We went through the other four bedrooms a bit more quickly. Each had a sign above the light switch with perfect little names.

The room with the tall four-post bed was called Luna. Whether it was a coincidence or the reason for its name, the full moon bathed the room in light from the massive windows. Bright white walls and bedding contrasted the dark wood floor and bedposts. A globe chandelier hung over the antique writing table next to the small wood-burning stove. The attached bathroom had a shower and a large full-length mirror.

Color practically burst from the room called Rainbow. The pink walls, flowery bedspread, and blue lampshades were only contrasted by the white fireplace and subway tile in the bathroom. Even the ceiling was a deep purple.

A muted gold bathed the walls and armchairs in Firefly. A bed with a huge wooden ornamental headboard was so tall I'd probably need a step-stool to get onto it. The stone fireplace had a decorative tile inlay depicting a swirl of tiny yellow fireflies. The bathroom was only big enough for an oversized tub and toilet, leaving the sink in the main bedroom area.

Exposed brick was the main focal point of the Borealis. If I didn't know I was on the upper level, I'd think we'd gone below ground with how cozy the room was. A brass-framed bed sat against the brick—a contrast in style that wasn't at all displeasing. Whoever had created these rooms deserved an award. They were like none other I'd seen in my life. The bathroom in the Borealis had its own fireplace, exposed beams on the ceiling, a claw-foot tub, and a little shelf filled with books.

Finally, we reached the room at the end of the hall. The door was closed with a wreath of what looked like fresh lilac hanging on the outside. I touched the petals gently and leaned closer to smell them. They were real.

"Ty went through a lot of trouble to make us feel welcome when we got here," I said to Penelope. "I mean, the flowers in each of the rooms were nice, but a lilac wreath? That's something I've never seen before."

Penelope gave me a tired oink.

The antique knob turned easily, and the heavy door swung open, revealing the master suite.

Esme's room.

The master bedroom was not named with a metal-stamped sign.

A large bed with a white-washed wood plank head-board sat against a light gray accent wall. Bookshelves bursting with books lined the opposite wall. The grandest fireplace I'd seen in any of the rooms sat on one wall, and another smaller fireplace sat next to the tub in the over-sized bathroom. A wing-back chair and a small table by the window overlooked the farm which stretched further than I could see in the dark.

For a moment, I panicked. That was a lot of corn. Maybe I would need Ty's help after all. Especially if I was going to take a job at the café. But if I got the corn picked, I could sell it and make money without splitting the profits. Plus, I was up for a challenge. I could do it.

"We're waking up early tomorrow," I told Penelope. "We have some corn to harvest."

3

I tried to sleep in Borealis, but by midnight, I was tired of tossing and turning. I felt like Esme would have wanted me to sleep in her room, but somehow it felt irreverent to do so.

So, in the middle of the night, I scooped up Penelope and headed out to sleep in Mona. Looking up through the skylight, I watched the stars until I drifted off to sleep.

It was still dark when I woke.

"Come on, Penelope, we need to get started on that corn."

Penelope was not interested in getting out of bed but eventually followed me outside.

The two of us walked up and down row after row of corn, gathering each odd-shaped cob into baskets. After every row, we had to take the baskets back to the porch to empty them. And we were on the short side of the field.

I had my work cut out for me.

Penelope was only too happy to curl up and go back to

sleep in the large sitting room when I hopped in the shower on the main level.

I hadn't cleaned Ty's room but made a mental note to do so the second I had a chance. I wasn't the cleanest person, but I couldn't let Esme down. She kept the house spotless, and I would do the same.

Mona didn't like early mornings any more than Penelope. When I cranked the engine, she acted as if she wouldn't start.

"Come on, girl. We need to get to town to get a job."

I turned the key in the ignition again, and she finally sputtered to life.

"Thank you."

She replied with a nearly empty gas gauge and an oil pressure warning light.

"Oh, Mona," I said. "You're so moody in the morning." I hugged the steering wheel, and the warning light flickered off. "That's better."

We made it to town just before the café opened. A group of older men in jeans and worn-out baseball caps stood off to the side as a woman unlocked the door. I pulled into an open parking space and turned off the engine. "If I get any tips," I told Mona, "I'll get you some gas before we head back to the house."

Katie's Café—a small blue building with white scalloped shutters—sat on the corner of a street lined with adorable shops. Next door, Amy's Antiques boasted a beautiful fall window display with pumpkins intermingled between old tricycles, dinnerware, and lamps providing a golden glow. Then there were Helen's Hardware, Nancy's Nails, and Belinda's B&B. The shops continued around a square with a sweet white gazebo sitting in the middle of a park full of lush green grass dotted with fall leaves from several humongous trees.

"Isn't it beautiful, Mona?" I sighed. Colorado was breathtaking with the mountains and the blue skies, but this charming town already felt more like home than Colorado ever had. Almost like it was where my heart yearned to be my entire life.

Five pickup trucks and a small car were parked in front of the café. Four of the trucks looked like farm trucks with toolboxes in the back. The fifth had a logo on the side that said Des Moines Developers. If I had to guess, that was the company trying to take over cornfields from the news the night before. Maybe the fashion lady from the TV was in town.

The sidewalk was empty—all the men had followed the woman inside. When I pulled open the heavy wooden door, sleigh bells rang, and the scent of bacon and coffee made my stomach grumble. I could only hope meals were a job perk. I was running low on Ty's peanut butter and bread.

"You can sit wherever," the woman who had opened the door said. She was my age, had curly black hair, and a smile that wouldn't indicate it was still before sunrise.

"I'm here to talk to Bex." Every head in the place turned my way. Which consisted of only Bex and the four men she was pouring coffee for. My scalp tingled, but I pushed the feeling away. I'd mastered my hair in most situations.

"You must be Ellie." She put the last cup of coffee on

the table and returned the pot to the industrial-sized machine. "I didn't expect you to be here so early."

"I wasn't sure when to come. Ty just told me to meet you."

"Have you ever waited tables before?"

"Once for about a month." I left out the part where I'd dumped an entire tray of meals on a table of eight. Thankfully, the shattered shards of the plates didn't hurt anyone. I might have kept the job if it hadn't been for the extreme embarrassment that caused my hair to frizz up into a bright blue puffball.

Okay, so maybe I hadn't *quite* mastered my hair.

I was working on it.

"Good enough for me." She handed me a ticket book, a pen, and a slim black apron from behind the cash register pedestal. "You keep your tips and get one meal when we're slow."

I could have cried. Gas money *and* a warm meal. "Thank you."

"Why don't you start with the farmers. They're tough, but once you get to know their orders, it'll make things much easier for you." She walked me over to a circular table with five chairs, one of them empty. "This is Ellie. She's going to take your order today."

"We haven't had our order taken once the past ten years." A man with a long white beard and tattooed sleeves who looked like a rock 'n roll Santa Claus said.

"This is Hank," she said to me, then turned to him. "I haven't been here ten years."

"It's been at least nine and a half," a man with glasses

so thick they made his eyes appear a few sizes larger than usual said.

"If you must know," Bex said. "It's been seven. But I started when I was in high school, so I'm not as old as you hooligans are implying."

They laughed.

Well, three of them laughed.

The fourth, who had neither spoken nor looked up from his paper, made no acknowledgment at all. With his distinguished salt and pepper hair and beard, he was the most handsome of all the older men, though he might have been more attractive with a smile or even a bit of eye contact.

"Now, you be nice to Ellie, or I'll tell your wives." Bex patted me on the back and left to greet a couple who walked through the door.

I fumbled to get my pen and pad ready. "So—uh—what can I get for you today?"

They each rattled off their orders—some pickier than others—until I got to the man with the paper.

"And for you?"

Hank nudged him in the side. "Give her your order."

The man looked up—his eyes almost gray. "Dry wheat toast and two slices of extra crispy bacon." He dropped his gaze back to the paper.

I double-checked their orders, reading them aloud to make sure I got it all right, then walked back into the kitchen.

Bex took the ticket and read it over. "Good job. You even got Earl's right. We'll work on the shorthand of it when you get to know the menu better." She slid the ticket onto a shelf that separated the cooking area with big flat cooktops from the walkway and dishwashing station. "Hey guys, this is Ellie. She's going to work with us now."

Two men turned from the grill.

"This is Big Charley and Little Charlie—for obvious reasons." Bex laughed.

"It's nice to meet you," I said.

"You're Esme's granddaughter, right?" Big Charley asked. He looked like he could have been the same age as I assumed Esme was.

"I am."

"Good woman, that one." He frowned. "I'm glad you made it here."

I was about to ask him if he had known my mother, but the bells on the door rang.

"Let's see who came in," Bex said.

I followed her into a whirlwind of a morning. By the time I caught my breath, I felt like I'd met everyone in town. Not that I'd remember any of their names.

"Now would be the time to get some food and take a break," Bex said when there was a lull in the activity. "You did good. It was nice having some help with the morning rush."

I sat down with a massive plate of pancakes and a fragrant cup of coffee and ate like my life depended on it. The crunchy bits on the side of the pancake were my favorite, almost like pancake cookies. Little Charlie tried to convince me to get the bacon, but I'd never be able to look Penelope in the eye again if I did.

The only two men left at the farmer's table were Hank and Earl. I wasn't usually one to listen in on other people's conversations, but it was hard not to hear what they were talking about.

"I saw Melody on TV last night," Hank said. "That two-hour special."

Earl just grunted.

"She's very talented," Hank said. "The way she did that spinning kickflip thing at the beginning was amazing. I hadn't seen that in any of the other episodes."

"I'm sure she has a stunt-double," Earl grumbled.

Hank took a drink of his coffee, then changed the subject. "Have you seen Percy since the incident?"

Earl leaned back in his chair, arching his back, a wince passing over his face. "He's probably still licking his wounds."

"Not like him to miss morning coffee. His field hasn't been harvested."

"Your field isn't harvested yet either," Earl said.

"Ty's working on it."

My ears perked up at the mention of Ty. Maybe Hank was his father? Or grandfather?

"Ty's lazy. He can't just bat his eyes at the field, and it'll magically be harvested. How's he going to manage when you keel over? He's going to inherit all that land and not know what to do with it."

I half expected Hank to defend Ty, but instead, he just said, "I'm not plannin' on keeling over anytime soon."

Earl looked like he wanted to say more, but he pushed his way to a stand. A definite look of pain crossed his face.

"You all right?" Hank said.

"I'm fine," Earl snapped. "Just sore from sitting in a

tractor all day. Not all of us have kids to do our work for us."

He obviously wasn't fine—emotionally or physically. He practically hobbled out of the café. He was the exact type of person Relief with Ellie was created to help. The only problem was, he'd have to be open to the help. And I was guessing he wasn't that kind of man.

When I looked back, Hank was staring right at me.

"You know, if Earl catches you listenin' to his conversations, you'll be out of a job quicker than you were hired."

I felt a blush travel up the back of my neck. "Sorry, I wasn't trying to—"

"Don't worry about it," he said, approaching the back booth where Bex told me to eat. "I don't mind you listening. How else will you know what's going on in town?"

"Are you related to Ty?" I asked.

"He's my boy," Hank said. "The wife and I didn't think we'd be able to have kids. Then boom, we turn fifty, and out he comes."

"For what it's worth," I said. "He was a perfect gentleman last night when I got to Esme's house."

"You mean your house," Hank said.

I shrugged. "I suppose so."

"You should be proud of it. A lot of people hoped that house would go on the market. Ty included."

"Ty wanted to buy Esme's—I mean—my house?"

"I suppose he didn't want to *buy* it," Hank said. "He probably thought it would be gifted to him when she passed."

"Oh," I said, feeling slightly guilty.

"Don't you think anything of it," Hank said. "Ty has plenty coming to him. Our family has a great deal of land, and he's the only child between my sister and me." The expression on Hank's face told me he wasn't entirely at ease with that transition. But he probably just didn't want to think about dying. "Ty tells me you're going to harvest the corn yourself?"

"I'm sorry," I said. "I wish I could let Ty help. But I'm going to need all the income I can get."

"I understand," he said, dropping a twenty-dollar bill on the table in front of me. "You did a good job today with our table. Those guys don't usually tip much, but I'll take care of you." He winked and walked out the door waving to Bex on the way out.

"Hank's a great guy," Bex said. "Always leaves the best tips."

"We can split it since you got them coffee," I said.

"Nope," she said. "No splitting tips, remember? Katie's rules. You earned that twenty."

"Speaking of Katie, when do I meet her?" I assumed Katie was the owner.

"Katie doesn't come in much anymore. She's left the business running to me." The pride in her voice was unmistakable. "But if she does, I'll introduce the two of you."

If Katie didn't run the café, did Amy run the antique store? Or Nancy the nail place? I had a lot to learn about Cliff Haven.

4

The café closed at two, and by the time I'd finished for the day, I'd made fifty-three dollars in tips. Bex asked me to come back Friday to start my scheduled days of Friday through Tuesday.

The sun shone brightly, making the reds and oranges of the leaves that still hung onto the tree branches shimmer. The walk to the bank was short but enjoyable with the fresh air and sound of birds chirping.

The documents were in the brown leather satchel with hearts and stars stamped into it I'd gotten from Santa over ten years ago. Of course, I knew it wasn't really from Santa, but my foster parents had done such a good job of acting, I almost believed them.

As far as the documents went, I'd tried to read through them, but the legalese made my head spin. Most of it seemed to be deeds and property specs—important to have, but not necessarily important to read. Which meant the best place for them would be in a safe deposit box in the bank. At least until I could afford an attorney to look them over.

The bank—Cliff Haven Municipal Bank—was only big enough to have two teller windows and a small lobby with a pedestal in the center for signing checks and such.

"Hi," I said. "I'd like to get a safe deposit box, please."

The woman across the counter was probably in her mid-forties with long brown hair, frumpy clothes, and a grumpy face. "What size?"

"Large enough to hold some documents." I held up the envelope.

"I heard you'd come to town," Sally—as her nametag indicated—said. "A box that size will be fifty dollars."

"A month?" I nearly swallowed my tongue.

"A year, but it's due upfront."

I pulled the cash from my pocket.

"Good tip day, huh?" Her tone wasn't friendly.

I handed her the fifty dollars and shoved the three back into my pocket. At least it would get me enough gas to get back to the house. I'd just have to make do with the peanut butter that was left.

"Fill out these papers." She pushed a form across the counter and disappeared into the back room.

She came back with a long metal box specifically created for documents. "Put your items inside."

I opened the box and inserted the papers while she looked over the form.

"Here's your key," she said. "The bank has one too, but your property will never be opened without your say-so. If you die, your property will be passed along to whoever you list in your will. If you do not have a will, it will be passed on to your next of kin."

I wanted to ask what happened if I had no next of kin, but if I were dead, it wouldn't really matter.

I locked the box and slid it back toward her.

"Is there anything else I can help you with today, Miss Vanderwick?"

"No, thank you." I smiled, trying to get her to smile back, but she didn't.

She didn't respond at all, just turned away with the box.

I shrugged and made my way toward the door.

"Oh, and Ellie?" the woman said from behind me.

I turned back. "Yes?"

"Stay away from Ty."

Did she think Ty and I had some sort of relationship? I had been in town less than twenty-four hours. "Ty and I only just met."

She frowned. "Stay away from Ty. If you know what's good for you."

I felt like my head was on fire. Thankfully, she had disappeared into the back room. I closed my eyes and took a few deep breaths before checking in the glass door to make sure my hair hadn't worked itself up into a tizzy. It was still in the ponytail I'd pulled it into before leaving the house. And still white as far as I could tell.

"Three dollars should get us just enough gas," I said to Mona when I got behind the wheel. She roared to life, eager to take me to the gas station. "Just remind me to steer clear of the bank unless absolutely necessary. I think one of the tellers has it out for me."

I parked Mona in the garage, and then Penelope and I worked through the rest of the afternoon into evening picking corn. By the time dinner came, I couldn't wait to have some fruit—or rather, vegetables—of our labor. It dawned on me halfway up one row that I had a feast right here. It wouldn't take away too many profits to boil up some corn. We'd have a corn and peanut butter sandwich on the cute back porch.

In theory, it would have been perfect. But the minute I bit into the corn, I knew something was wrong. It was dry and flavorless, making my mouth feel like I'd shoved it full of cotton balls. I spit it into a napkin and then took Penelope's off her plate. "Sorry, sweetie. I don't think this corn is good."

I looked around at all the corn we'd gathered. If the corn was bad—which it very obviously was—I wouldn't make a profit. Cool tingles like those from an icy rain storm pricked at my scalp, and I let the emotion take over.

Sadness was my least favorite emotion, but sometimes I had to let myself be sad. At least, that's what one of my therapists told me as a child. One of the better foster families had taken me to a sweet young woman who gave me candy and let me show her my fledgling yoga moves as long as I talked to her about my emotions. It was one of the rare moments I'd let my guard down in hopes I'd be accepted.

Then my hair turned bright pink, and she did what most people did—freaked out. I didn't stay with that family much longer. It wasn't every day a young girl could scare the daylights out of a trained therapist.

"What are we going to do with all this corn?" I asked Penelope.

She nudged me with her peanut butter covered snout.

"You're right," I said. "Maybe we just got a bad batch. Maybe the small part of the field didn't get the right amount of rain or sun or something. Tomorrow, we'll work on picking the big field."

Penelope let out a little grunt, and I could feel my hair returning to normal. Everything was going to be okay. I just had to put in the work.

5

After trying another room—Rainbow—and ending up in Mona again, Penelope and I spent the next morning in the field. The sun shone overhead, causing tiny trails of sweat to weave their way down my back like snowboarders down a ski slope. We'd made some progress on the big field, but if we were going to get all the corn harvested before the snow hit, we'd need to pick up the pace.

"Should we go inside and try some of this corn for lunch?" I asked when my legs felt like they were about to give out.

Penelope oinked her happy little oink and took off toward the house. Hopefully, the corn was good because we'd nearly finished the peanut butter and bread earlier that morning.

A terrified squeal ahead made my tired legs kick into sprinter mode. Something was wrong with Penelope.

I tore through the rows to get to where she was squealing and turning around in circles. I scooped her up into my arms before I found what she was worked up about.

A man was lying face-down in between two rows of corn.

My scalp erupted in heat as if my head had been doused in gasoline and someone lit a match.

I glanced around but saw no one.

Maybe he was just sleeping. Please, let him be sleeping.

I nudged his boot with the tip of my sneaker. "Hello, there. Are you okay?"

No response.

Penelope looked up at me knowingly.

"He can't be. There has to be a reasonable explanation."

I bent down and placed two of my fingers on the side of his neck like I'd learned in the CPR class I'd taken for a camp counselor position in Colorado.

Not only did he have no pulse, his body was cold.

I yanked my fingers away and steadied myself.

There was a dead man in my cornfield.

I tried to make a mental note of where the body was before I ran to the garage.

I'd plugged my phone in on Mona's dash. Most of the time, I didn't take it with me. It wasn't like Penelope could call me. No one besides my ex-boyfriends had the number, and I was pretty sure none of them would call.

"9-1-1, what's your location?" The dispatcher said.

I tried to remember the address of Esme's house. "I'm not completely sure," I said. "I'm sorry. I'm new here. Do you know Esme Vanderwick's house?"

"Sure thing," she said, her tone kind and calm. "And with whom am I speaking?"

"Ellie Vanderwick."

"Ms. Vanderwick, what's the nature of your emergency?"

"I think—no—I'm sure, there's a dead body in my cornfield."

"I'm sorry, can you say that again?" she said. "I think I may have heard you wrong."

"There's a dead body in my cornfield," I said as clearly as I could.

The line was silent for a moment. "Dead. Are you sure the person is dead?"

"He has no pulse."

"Please hold on the line while I get an officer en route to your location."

"Thank you." I switched my phone to speaker and laid it on the countertop in the back of Mona while I fumbled around to get a scarf. One glance in the rearview mirror told me what I could have guessed. My hair had pulled itself into curls so tight my head would ache for days, which wouldn't have been a problem, except now my hair was also jet black.

"Are you still there?" the dispatcher asked.

"Yes, ma'am." I checked in a handheld mirror to make sure I'd tucked in all the curly black pieces.

"Officers should be there shortly. If you need anything else, please call us back."

A police car was pulling in as I was disconnecting the call. A man and a woman approached as I walked out of the garage. I reached a hand up to my hair to make sure the scarf stayed in place.

The man—probably in his forties—was tall with broad shoulders and a pensive look on his face. The woman—older, maybe in her fifties—was short but looked tough.

"I hear you have a body on your hands?" the man said. When he took off his sunglasses, he met me with a set of light blue eyes I'd only ever seen once.

In the mirror.

My breath caught in my chest, sending my scalp into a renewed fit of fire. What if this man was my father?

"I'm Police Chief Jake Mulroney, and this is Officer Deb Jones."

I couldn't find any words. Did he see it too? If he did, he wasn't letting on.

"Okay," Jake said, probably confused by my silence. "Would you like to take us to the body?"

He said it as if he didn't believe me. Then the words from Esme's letter popped into my mind. This town had hardly any crime.

Until I got here.

But maybe this wasn't a crime. Maybe the man had died of natural causes.

I lead the two officers through the corn as best as I could remember. "I'm Ellie Vanderwick," I finally said. "Esme's granddaughter."

I peeked over my shoulder to see if Jake reacted, but his expression remained neutral.

"It's really too bad about Esme," Deb said.

I walked through one more row and almost stepped directly on the dead man's hand. I averted my eyes.

"It's Percy," Deb said in a hushed voice as she checked for a pulse.

Percy.

As in the Percy Earl and Hank were talking about at the café?

"I'll call it in," Deb said, leaving Jake and me alone with the body.

"If you want to wait in the house, you can," Jake said. "But we will have some questions for you." He didn't look at me. Whatever resemblance we had was probably in my imagination. My mind was grasping for something—anything—that would reveal my history.

"Just let me know if you need anything," I said before walking back.

Deb was by the police car when a massive tractor came trundling up the driveway. It had huge pointy teeth on the front pointing at me as if they might stab me in the chest if I came too close.

When the engine sputtered to a stop, Ty jumped down from the cab.

"What are you doing here?" Deb asked.

"I'm here to cut the corn," he said.

"Why?" I asked, walking up beside them. "I thought I told you I could do it myself."

"You still think you can do it yourself?" He grinned, showing his perfectly white teeth.

"I did all that." I pointed to the wrap-around porch and the piles of corn. "But the stuff on that side's bad."

"It's bad?" Ty asked.

"Penelope and I had some for dinner last night. We spit it out pretty quickly." The image of the man lying in my cornfield popped into my head. "Maybe," I said to Deb, "that man ate my corn, and it killed him."

Guilt rose inside me. I hadn't been here a week, and I was already responsible for someone's death. I was just lucky Penelope and I hadn't eaten any.

"Killed who?" Ty asked.

"This is police business," Deb interjected. "We'll issue a statement after the family has been notified."

"Oh, come on," Ty said, smiling at her. "You can trust me."

The smile didn't have the desired effect on Deb. She shook her head. "I don't know that I can."

"What's that supposed to mean?" Ty said.

"I think you know." She pushed past him to meet the ambulance driving through my lawn to get around the tractor Ty left in the middle of the driveway.

"Go move your tractor," I said. "They're driving on my grass."

"*Your* grass, huh?" He raised an eyebrow.

Guilt tore through me. Here I was practically boasting about this new property I'd inherited from a woman I'd never known when the man who was practically her grandson had gotten nothing.

"Don't worry, they won't hurt your grass," he said. "It's not like weak Colorado grass. Our grass is resilient."

Resilient or not, it was still rude to drive on someone's lawn. I'd never felt so protective about anything other than Penelope and Mona before.

"So, who's the dead guy?" Ty asked, smiling as if I was the only person in the entire world.

Something in me wanted to tell him. But I shook my head. "I probably shouldn't answer that."

"Oh, come on. Deb doesn't know what she's talking about," he said. "I am very trustworthy."

"I need to get back inside." If I stayed out there any longer, I was going to tell him. "Jake wants to talk to me after they're done."

I didn't wait for his approval, but I felt his gaze on me as I walked back to the house.

6

Inside it was cool, but the air was stagnant. I needed a breeze.

I turned off the air conditioner and opened all the windows.

"Penelope?"

She ran inside through the dog—or rather, piggy—door when I'd called the police.

I looked up the stairs, and there she was, lying at the top. Penelope could climb stairs pretty easily, but coming back down wasn't her favorite thing to do.

"It's okay. The police took over." I marched up, gathered her in my arms, and carried her back down to the sitting room where the breeze blew the sheer white curtains like dancing ghosts.

"Why are you here?" A man said outside. I peeked out the window to find Hank talking to Ty. "She told you she didn't want your help. Were you just going to harvest the corn without her say-so?"

"Two days ago, I wouldn't have needed her say-so. For years, I've tended this farm."

"But now, it's hers, son," Hank said. "No matter how hard it is, you have to come to terms with it."

There was that guilt again.

"She's going to need my help." Ty kicked at the gravel. "There's no way she can pick all that corn by hand."

"Looks like she's made some progress." Hank motioned toward the porch.

I ducked out of sight, hoping he hadn't seen me.

"You and I both know picking corn by hand won't work. She'll come crawling back soon."

"She doesn't seem like the type to crawl back to anyone." Hank laughed. "But if she's anything like Esme, she'll know when to ask for help. And when she does, make sure you're not using the chopping head."

Ty whipped around toward the cornfield, his face not the confident one he usually had.

Hank was right. I would need help. It was probably best to just ask for it while they were there rather than making them come back.

I got up, leaving Penelope to curl up in the chair. "I'll be right back."

When Hank saw me coming, he smiled. "How you doing, kiddo? I heard about what you found."

"I'm okay. I feel terrible. I hope it wasn't the corn."

"Your corn didn't kill him," Ty practically shouted, though I was only a few feet from him. "Your corn is fine." He took a breath and softened his tone. "You're not supposed to eat it. It's field corn. We use it for feed and ethanol and a bunch of other things."

"That's good to know," I said, trying not to let his attitude affect me. He was likely just getting out his pent-up frustration from me getting what was rightfully his. "I guess, since it's not bad, I might take you up on your offer to harvest it. If you're still willing."

Hank smiled at Ty in an I-told-you-so way.

"Yeah, for sure," Ty said.

"No one's harvesting that corn until we can fully process the crime scene," Jake said, walking up behind us.

"Crime scene?" I asked.

"Just a precaution," Deb said. "We're not implying anything."

"Right," Jake said. "A . . . precaution."

"You don't think someone intentionally killed another person in Cliff Haven, do you?" Hank asked.

"Just doing our due diligence," Jake said. "Until the coroner does the official autopsy, we won't know."

"And you're sure it wasn't the corn?" I asked.

"Why would you think it would be the corn?" Jake asked, finally looking at me.

"She ate some and thought it was poisoned." Deb smiled. "It's okay. If you're not around it, you probably didn't know. But no, it's highly unlikely your corn was the reason for his death."

"Your presence on the other hand . . ." Sally, from the bank, came walking up next to Ty and slipped an arm around his waist. Ah, so that's why she told me to stay away from him. I hadn't even heard her pull in the driveway.

"Sally," Hank chided.

"What?" she said. "There hasn't been a murder in Cliff

Haven for years. Then she shows up and, boom, someone's dead in her cornfield. Bet it was Percy. Rumor is he hasn't been home for a week."

"Uncle Percy?" Ty said, his face full of shock.

"That's why rumors shouldn't be trusted," Hank said. "I saw Percy at the café three mornings ago."

Jake scribbled in a notepad he'd pulled from his chest pocket. "Anything else?" He looked up at the group of us.

"If it is Percy—" Hank cleared his throat and pulled his cap from his head, revealing more white hair to match his beard. "—I should probably tell you about the incident."

"Go on," Jake said.

"Not yesterday, but uh, Tuesday afternoon, he was down at Fran's picking up some feed for his chickens and got into an argument with Earl." Hank scratched the top of his head, still holding the bill of his hat in his hand. "Not saying Earl would kill him, but maybe things got out of hand."

"Do you know what the argument was about?" Jake asked.

"Same stuff. Property line, neighbors, you know," Hank said. "Percy and Earl didn't see eye to eye. They were always getting into arguments."

"I heard this last one was a doozy, though," Sally said. "They were throwing stuff all over the place. Fran was beside herself when she told me about it at the bank the next day."

Jake nodded. "Anything else?"

"Not that I can think of," Hank said. "But if it's all right with you, I'd like to tell Helen her husband's gone."

Jake nodded.

"When do you think I can harvest the corn?" Ty asked.

"You can harvest most of it, just don't cross the police tape lines we set up," Deb said. "We should have the scene processed by the end of the day tomorrow."

As if on cue, the ambulance came rolling out from behind the house. Ty took off his hat—Hank's was already off—as we watched it approach.

"Can I ask you a couple of questions?" Jake asked me.

"Sure," I said. "Should we go inside?"

He nodded, and I turned and walked toward the house.

Behind me, I could hear Ty say, "I'm going to take the tractor home, take off the chopping head, and come back to harvest what I can."

"Want me to come with you?" Sally asked.

I didn't hear Ty's response. I glanced back to see him getting into the cab of the tractor and Sally looking up at him with her hands on her hips.

"They make an odd couple," Jake said as if reading my mind. "But they've been together on and off a long time—practically since he turned eighteen. I think they were even engaged at one point." He shook his head. "I don't know. It's hard to keep up."

Sounded creepy. She was old enough to be his mother.

Penelope perked up when we walked in the door. I gathered her up off the chair and took her to the dining room.

"Who's this little lady?" Jake asked, scratching Penelope under her chin.

"Her name's Penelope," I said. "She found me a few years ago."

"Pigs are so much smarter than people give them

credit for." He bent over and looked her in the eye. "And cuter too."

"Are you thirsty?" I asked. "I have water if you'd like something to drink. The ice machine works."

"Water would be great," Jake said. "Is the AC broken?" He had a couple of small beads of sweat on his forehead below his dark brown hair.

We went into the kitchen, and I poured him a glass of ice water. "I just thought it would be nice to get a breeze through the house. It was getting stagnant in here."

He took a big drink and sighed. "It's a hot one today. Esme always had the windows open too." He smiled. "Even when it was a million degrees with a hundred percent humidity. But the house was never this clean." He looked around the kitchen as if he were inspecting it.

Every little tidbit I learned about Esme had a double effect—first, I was warm and fuzzy inside, then I yearned for more. "Were you and Esme close?"

"Esme was close with everyone in Cliff Haven. She was the heart of the town." He motioned to the knife block on the countertop. "Do you mind if I look at these?"

"Sure," I said. What did it matter to me whether he looked at the knives?

"Did you clean the house, or was it like this when you got here?" He pulled each knife out and examined it before replacing it in the block.

"It was like this," I said. "Pretty much perfect, other than the room where Ty stayed. He left in a hurry."

Jake nodded. "Have you cleaned it since?"

I blushed. "I haven't really had a chance."

"That's okay," he said. "Do you mind if I take a look?"

"Be my guest."

I followed him upstairs, anticipation building in my chest. I desperately wanted to ask him about my mother. Whether they knew each other. Whether he was my father.

He ran a hand through his feathery hair as we reached Dewdrop.

"You haven't touched anything?" he asked.

"Only the TV—I turned it off," I said. "Do you think Ty had something to do with his uncle's death?"

"Just covering the bases. He has a pretty solid alibi, so it's unlikely." He pulled on a pair of gloves and stepped inside. "What was on the TV? Do you remember?"

I tried to remember that night. "The end of that super-hero show and the news," I said. "The nine o'clock news. A woman was talking about building modern housing in cornfields or something."

He lifted the sheets and glanced under the bed, apparently not finding anything. He moved to the closet and bathroom while I waited with a question stuck in the back of my throat.

When he walked out of the bathroom, and his gaze met mine, my mouth acted on its own accord. "Did you know my mother?"

Jake paused like I'd slapped him across the face. Then his features softened. "I did," he finally said.

"Were you—"

"Just acquaintances."

My heart sank.

I didn't know Jake from any random man on the street. I didn't know if he was a decent human being. If he liked jam or jelly. If he had to work out to stay fit, or if he was just naturally in shape. But none of those things would have mattered if he'd told me he was my father.

"Do you know anyone who might have known my mother more . . . closely?" I almost said intimately, but I didn't want to sound weird.

"I can ask around," he said with a shrug. "So that night, how long before you turned off the TV did you arrive?"

"A half-hour, maybe," I said, trying to keep the disappointment out of my voice from being brushed off. "We came in. Ty came downstairs." I left out the towel part. "And then went back upstairs to—uh—pack. While he was gone, Penelope and I ate peanut butter sandwiches. He came back down and left, and Penelope and I went upstairs to check out the place."

"Ty was alone in the house?"

"As far as I know," I said. "But I guess someone else could have been here."

Jake nodded. "And did you see or hear anything strange that night?"

I shook my head. "Not really. We ended up sleeping in Mona—"

"Mona?"

"My van," I said. "She's been my home on and off since I bought her when I was seventeen."

"Why didn't you sleep inside?" He glanced around. "This house has plenty of rooms."

I glanced down the hallway. "I guess we just haven't

found the right one yet."

"Why didn't you take the master bedroom?"

I wrapped my arms around myself, though I wasn't cold. "It just seems disrespectful."

"I assure you," he said. "If Esme were alive, she'd want nothing more."

I didn't reply. She might have, but I still didn't feel like this was my house.

"You're working down at the café, right?" Jake started walking back down the hallway toward the stairs.

"I am," I said.

"Did you hear any gossip while you were there?"

"Nothing more than what Hank told you outside. There was an incident, and Percy hadn't been to coffee or harvested his field."

"He hasn't harvested yet, huh?"

"That's what Earl said."

"Is there anything else you can remember? Or any . . . feeling about what might have happened?"

I shook my head. "No, but if I do, I'll let you know."

He handed me a business card when we were at the bottom of the stairs.

"Please do," he said. "And whatever you do, don't eat any more of the corn."

I laughed, but my stomach growled. If only I hadn't opened that account, I'd be eating steak for dinner. But the documents needed to be kept safe.

Jake was at the door when I asked him one last question. "What was her name?"

He stopped, his hand outstretched toward the handle.

"Emily," he whispered, then turned. "Her name was Emily."

For a second, I thought I saw a glint of something in his eye, but then he pushed his way out the door and was gone.

7

Just as quickly as everyone had come, they were gone, leaving Penelope and me to ourselves. I pulled the scarf from around my hair. It was almost like it exhaled, draping down around my shoulders in loose white waves.

Back to normal.

Penelope oinked up at me.

"I bet you're hungry, aren't you?"

She practically ran to the kitchen.

There was only one slice of bread and the smallest bit of peanut butter left. My stomach grumbled, but I could go without. Penelope couldn't. I smeared the last of the peanut butter onto the piece of bread and handed it down to her.

She looked up at me as if asking if I was sure.

"Go ahead. You eat it. I work tomorrow. I'll get food then."

Penelope didn't hesitate another moment. She gobbled

it up, leaving the faintest smudge of peanut butter on her snout. I wiped it clean. "Feel better?"

Penelope let out a low oink.

"Me neither." I sighed then an idea popped into my head. "Let's take a walk."

Penelope practically hopped straight up in the air. She loved walks.

She stood still as a statue while I snapped on her pink sparkly harness and attached the matching leash.

On our walk, I thought about Percy's death. How he was just lying there as if asleep. Had someone killed him? Was it Ty?

No, Jake said Ty had an alibi.

If it wasn't Ty, then who was it?

I shook my head to clear my thoughts. I was not a police officer. I had no business getting in the middle of a murder investigation.

I was lost in thought when I heard the rumble approaching from behind. I glanced over my shoulder just in time to see a big red pickup barreling toward us. I grabbed Penelope and jumped into the ditch before the truck completely ran us over.

"Are you okay?" I coughed at the dust cloud from the gravel road.

Penelope nuzzled into me.

"I'm okay." I stood and wiped off my butt. "Just a couple of scrapes. No blood."

I looked both ways before continuing on the road. Had they not seen us? Was that even possible?

Maybe they were texting. Which reminded me I'd left my phone at home.

Home.

Just the thought made me warm inside. I had a home.

At the bend in the road, a gravel driveway led to a small but pretty green house. It might have blended into the corn if it wasn't for the bright white shutters. Parked in front of the house were probably fifteen cars and trucks, including the red one that had run me off the road.

And stepping out of the driver's side of the truck was none other than Sally, the not-so-friendly bank teller dressed like she was headed into a night club. She wore a tight black skirt that went just past her butt and a long sleeve blouse that showed way too much cleavage. Her heels made her look six feet tall, and the diamonds on her wrist and neck sparkled in the sunlight.

I had half a mind to march up to her and demand an apology. But it wouldn't do me any good stirring up drama.

Instinctively, I dodged out of the road when I heard another vehicle approaching. But when I turned, a car was slowing to a stop next to me.

The window rolled down, and I peeked inside.

"Out walking little miss bacon, huh?" Bex laughed.

If anyone else had called Penelope bacon, I might have been irritated, but Bex said it in a way that made it sound like a term of endearment.

"Yep," I said. "What's going on here? Some kind of party?"

"This is Helen and Percy's place. The town closed down so we could help. Wanna join?"

"Sure," I said. "If you think it's okay that Penelope comes too?"

"I'm sure she'll be more than welcome." Bex eased off the brake and inched forward. "Do you want a ride?"

"Nah, I'll meet you up there." It was only a few more yards to the house.

Bex waited for me by her car.

"Did you think I was going to hit you back there?" she asked.

"I wasn't sure," I said. "Sally would have if I hadn't jumped in the ditch."

"Sally's a terrible driver," Bex said. "And not someone you want to mess with."

She added the last part almost as if she knew I'd had thoughts about giving Sally a piece of my mind.

"Good to know." We walked toward the house together.

"Sorry you had to find Percy like that," Bex said. "I can't imagine how hard that must have been."

"I'd never met him, so it wasn't as bad as it could have been." I picked up Penelope before we got to the doors. I didn't know how Helen would feel about a pig walking into her house. "I just feel bad for the community."

Bex stopped at the top step. "I just can't believe anyone killed him. He was the nicest man on the planet. His and Helen's love story was practically a fairy tale."

She wiped a tear from her eye and opened the door.

The first person I made eye contact with was Sally, and she was glaring.

I turned to Bex. "I forgot to ask, why is she dressed like that?" Everyone else was wearing normal everyday clothes.

"She always looks like that when she's not at the

bank," Bex said. "Besides the jewelry. It changes on the regular."

I glanced around the room to see a couple of teenagers sitting on the couches, a group of gray-haired women standing near the back door, and a table full of mouth-watering food.

Bex walked straight toward the gray-haired women and grabbed one of their hands in her own.

"I am so sorry for your loss," she said.

"Thank you, dear," the woman—whose hands looked stronger than any grandma's hands I'd ever seen—said. "Won't you introduce me to your friend?"

"This is Ellie Vanderwick—Esme's granddaughter." Bex turned to me and said, "This is Helen, Percy's wife."

Tears filled Helen's eyes, and before I knew it, she had engulfed me in a hug of mass proportions. Helen's arms were tight around my neck, and all of the other women came up around us to join in.

Penelope squealed happily. She loved snuggles.

"And who do you have here?" Helen said, wiping tears away.

"This is Penelope," I said. "If you want me to take her outside, I can."

"Absolutely not," Helen said, patting Penelope on the head. "She's just as welcome as you are. Just don't let her get into the cabinets. I have some poison out for the mice."

I'd never had to worry about mice before—they didn't really have a chance to get into Mona with how much we moved around.

"I'm so sorry you weren't able to meet Esme before she passed," Helen said. "She was a dear friend of ours."

"I am too." I felt slightly guilty that we were talking about my loss when she had just lost her husband. "She sounds like she was a wonderful woman."

"She was more than wonderful," another woman with longer salt-and-pepper hair said. "She was everything. We miss her so much."

The other women nodded, dabbing their eyes with handkerchiefs.

"She would have loved you," a woman with a round face, rosy cheeks, and an ensemble made up of strictly red hues said. "She did love you."

"I have so many questions," I said. "I want to know everything."

My stomach growled loudly enough that even Penelope jumped.

"We'll have time for that later. First, we need to get you some food," Helen said. "You look like you haven't eaten in a month."

As a group, the women led me to the food and insisted I tried all their dishes. I agreed to everything except the pork tenderloin. The woman in red—Nancy—only looked slightly disappointed but seemed to understand when I explained I couldn't eat pork since my best friend in the entire world was a pig.

I finished all the food on my plate plus a huge glass of lemonade.

The conversation continued around me. Most people talked about Percy and what Helen was going to do now. I gathered from the chatter that Percy and Helen hadn't had any kids, though it sounded like they tried for years, Helen just couldn't get pregnant.

"Who's going to take care of the farm now?" I asked Bex.

"Hank," Bex said. "He's Helen's brother. His property is really just the other half of one big plot that Hank and Helen split when their folks died."

"Tell us the story again," Nancy said, sitting across from Helen.

Helen smiled, but it was tinged with sadness. "Which story?"

"You know which story." One of the older women with bright blue, dyed hair leaned forward eagerly. "The one about how you and Percy met."

Helen looked out the window and a smile—a real smile this time—washed over her face and created creases that only came from a life lived well.

"It was tenth grade," Helen said. "Percy was the new boy, and all the girls were excited to have a new love interest."

"Percy was quite the looker," Nancy said, nudging me in the side.

"And I was the nerd," Helen said. "I had braces, played tuba in the band, and wore glasses thicker than the bottom of coke bottles." Helen paused. "But Percy noticed me."

She stopped, and I thought for a moment that was the end of the story.

"I didn't know he noticed me—didn't expect it," Helen continued. "After all, it wasn't like I had boys breaking down my door like Katie or Esme." She glanced at me.

"Your grandmother was stunning. All the boys wanted to court her. But not my Percy. He only had eyes for me."

Nancy let out a sigh.

"It was the day of the homecoming dance," Helen said. "I wasn't planning to go. No one had asked me. I still had no idea Percy even knew I existed. In fact, Nancy and I were going to watch movies and eat popcorn."

"At least that's what you thought," Nancy said, wiggling her eyebrows.

"Yes, that's what I thought," Helen said. "But Nancy was in on the whole plot."

"What plot?" I asked, unable to resist.

Bex laughed. She'd obviously already heard this story.

"The plot to get Helen to the dance," Nancy said. "Percy asked for my help weeks before. We found a dress, shoes, and someone to do her hair and makeup."

"So when I arrived at Nancy's house dressed in sweats with my hair a frizzy mess, I didn't think much of it that her older sister was going to give us makeovers."

Nancy nodded. "She was in beauty school and needed the practice."

"She loved trying new things. Usually, I ended up looking like a street-walking poodle," Helen said. "But this time, when she handed me the mirror, I gasped."

Nancy had tears in her eyes. "She looked beautiful."

"I didn't even recognize myself," Helen said. "I think I remember talking about how it was too bad we weren't going to the dance after all."

"And that's when I suggested we dress up and take pictures with my mom's new camera," Nancy said.

"I should have been suspicious when you had a dress

and shoes in my size," Helen said. "Nancy was always at least a size smaller than me. And her feet are itsy bitsy."

Nancy shrugged.

"But I didn't think about it," Helen said. "I was just excited to look better than I ever had in my entire life." She wiped a tear that had dropped onto her cheek. "When we went upstairs to take pictures, Percy was sitting on the couch."

"She nearly fainted," Nancy said. "I had to hold her up."

"I thought for sure he was there for Nancy's sister or something," Helen said. "But when he stood and took my hand, I was in utter shock."

"As was he," Nancy said. "You looked completely different."

"His voice cracked when he asked if I wanted to go to the dance with him."

"She almost said no." Nancy shook her head with a smile. "But I made her."

"And it was magical," Helen said. "I felt like Cinderella."

"They've been inseparable since," Nancy said.

Helen's smile faded. "I'm sorry," she said. "Will you excuse me?"

She stood and made her way out of the room.

"I can't imagine losing Hank," Nancy said. "And our relationship isn't nearly as strong as Helen's and Percy's."

Bex nodded. "They're the perfect couple in every sense of the word."

"Speaking of Hank," I said. "Where is he?"

Nancy smiled. "How about I show you?"

8

Penelope and I followed Nancy out the back door, where I saw a breathtaking sight. Five giant tractors like the one Ty had been driving earlier drove toward us in a staggered line. The stalks of corn fed through the teeth like hair through a comb leaving a nearly smooth field behind.

"Here in Cliff Haven—or really, all of Iowa—we help each other," Nancy said. "These farmers would usually be harvesting their own fields, but they knew there was a need. And as they say, more hands make quicker work."

I suspected the size of the tractor helped too. Just the thought of me picking corn by hand made me cringe. Ty must have thought I was a complete idiot.

"Why does this field look so much different than the one across the street?" I asked.

Nancy looked at the field and the one across the street and then back again. "Oh, they just cut this one shorter with the chopping head. Different farmers like different things. I'm sure Hank and Earl could give you all the boring details if you wanted them."

I smiled.

"Here's another glass of lemonade," Bex said, appearing next to me.

The entire group of people from the house made their way out, and we watched the tractors work as the sunset painted the sky orange and pink and purple.

When the bugs started to bite, Helen said, "Let's go inside and get some dessert."

This elicited cheers from the group around me. Nancy wrapped an arm around my waist and ushered me inside. "Don't worry, there's no pig products in the desserts," she said, giving Penelope a little scratch behind the ear. "I think I know how you feel. If someone told me they wanted me to eat a fried Corgi sandwich, I'd pass out."

I laughed.

"What's so funny?" Sally asked, turning around to glare at me again.

"That's none of your business," Nancy said, her sweet old grandma façade changing into what seemed like protector mode as she placed herself between Sally and me.

Sally raised her hands in surrender. "Point taken. I'll butt out." She walked across the room to talk to a few other women around her age.

"That Sally is bad news," Nancy said. "I don't know why my Ty couldn't find a nice girl like you instead of that old lady."

I nearly laughed because Sally was much younger than

Nancy, but I guessed she was pretty old in terms of Ty's age.

When the back door opened and the farmers walked in, each of them went to their wives and gave them a kiss or hug or—in Hank's case—a slap on Nancy's butt. Nancy giggled and slapped his hand away. Ty rolled his eyes then smiled when his gaze met mine, but Sally yanked on his arm, drawing his attention back to her.

"Jake said Sally and Ty have been together a while," I said to Bex, frustration poking through my words. I couldn't believe I was letting some stupid attraction to Ty influence my mood. My scalp tingled, but this was the last place I could have my hair going all wonky.

"They're on again off again," Bex said. "Sally and Jake dated in high school. Sometimes she flirts with Jake to make Ty mad, but he couldn't care less. Ty's a total player. Sally may only have eyes for him, but he doesn't share the sentiment."

I watched as Ty hastily dropped spoonful after spoonful of different casseroles onto his wobbly paper plate as Sally looked on in disgust.

"Oh no," Bex said, reading the look on my face. "Do not get involved with Ty. He's nothing but trouble."

I glanced over at Bex.

"Just trust me. I know."

I laughed. "You dated him?"

"In high school." She nodded. "But even back then, he was a player. He cheated on me . . . with Sally."

"When he was in *high school*?" I gaped at her. "But that's—"

"Illegal," she said. "Yeah. And gross."

I looked over at Sally, her hand now brushing down Ty's back.

Ugh. That was so creepy.

"Can you tell me where the bathroom is?" I asked. Irritation was getting the best of me.

"Down the hall and to the right," Bex said. "You okay?"

"Yeah, I just need to freshen up," I said. "Can you hold Penelope?"

Bex pulled Penelope into her chest and kissed the top of her head.

When I got to the bathroom and glanced in the mirror, the only noticeable difference to my hair was that it was beginning to frizz, and my roots—which I didn't naturally have—were a light red. I took a deep breath and ran some cold water over my hands, then splashed it up onto my face. I guess this was one of those times it was good I couldn't afford makeup.

I grabbed a towel from the rack across from the toilet and wiped my face. When I inhaled, I nearly gagged. I pulled the towel away to find what looked like dried chunks of vomit.

I folded it so the vomit was on the inside and hung it back up. Then I rewashed my face, this time using the bottom of my tank top to dry it.

Helen didn't seem like the type to keep a dirty towel in her bathroom. The rest of her house was spotless. But she had just lost her husband.

I reached for the door but heard Sally's voice outside. I stopped. I didn't need another run-in with her. Not now. Not ever.

"All the money?" Another voice—a woman—said.

"Yep," Sally said. "Their account is empty."

"What did he do with it?"

"No idea. He'd come in every once in a while and make the withdrawal, but most of it came out of an ATM in Chicago."

"Maybe it was for the farm."

"Doubtful," Sally said. "I don't think Helen knows."

"She will when her mortgage comes due."

"Hopefully, he had life insurance," Sally said, then it was quiet.

I waited for a minute, checked my hair one last time to make sure the red was gone, and then stepped out.

"You okay?" Bex asked. "You look like something didn't hit you quite right. Was it the jalapeño peppers? They came straight from Nancy's garden."

"I'm good." I was still processing what I'd heard from the bathroom. When Helen met my gaze with a smile, I had to look away for fear she'd see the pity in my eyes. How horrible to have been lied to.

"Earth to, Ellie," Bex said. "Your momma's in her own little world, Bits," she said to Penelope.

Her comment snapped me back into the moment. "What did you call her?"

"Bits. Like the bacon kind. I thought it suited her better than Little Miss Bacon."

I shook my head and smiled. "Bits. I like it. Do you like it, Penelope?"

Penelope wiggled her snout.

"I think that's a yes," I said, and Bex and I laughed.

"Are you really going to be with her tonight?" Sally's

voice rose over the crowd as she pointed her finger directly at me.

A few gasps came from the older women.

Embarrassment flooded my cheeks. What was she talking about? Ty and I didn't have plans tonight or ever.

"It's a job," Ty said. "I'm harvesting her field."

Oh, that.

"Is that what you call it?" Sally said. "I can't believe you'd even step foot on that property after what she did."

"What are you talking about?" He brushed his shaggy hair out of his face.

Everyone was staring at me now. Tension built in my hair follicles. If this got worse, I'd need to get out of there. And fast.

"Don't you think it's weird that the minute she comes into town, someone dies? Someone's *murdered*?" She was practically screaming. "She murdered your uncle!"

And it got worse.

"I'm sorry, I need to leave," I said to no one and everyone. I took Penelope back from Bex and made my way to the back door.

"See, if she wasn't guilty, she wouldn't run," Sally's voice echoed behind me.

"I'm so sorry for your loss. Thank you for the food," I said to Helen before I burst out the door and started running.

I ran directly through Helen and Percy's freshly harvested field—careful to avoid the bits of cornstalk that still poked up from the ground—toward my house.

Tears flowed down my cheeks, and I would bet, if I

looked in a mirror, my hair would be completely out of control.

I could see the light on the barn through the cornstalks when I stopped dead in my tracks just before I toppled over the police tape.

In front of me was the crime scene—the place Percy had taken his last breath. A spray paint outline of his body was on the ground with a brown stain in the dirt right where his belly button would have been. I could still see his actual body in my mind, but I didn't remember seeing any blood.

How had he died? I glanced around for a clue. Had he been shot? Or stabbed? Is that why Jake had been looking through my knives?

Then I laughed to myself. The police would have found the evidence already.

I walked away from the scene, defeated. If people believed Sally that I'd somehow hurt Percy, I'd be an outcast before I'd ever get the chance to fit in. Before I reached the edge of the field, something on the ground caught my eye.

I picked up what looked like a torn piece of a t-shirt. I flipped it over in my hands. It wasn't terribly dirty, but my mind was telling me to smell it, for some awful reason.

I shook my head. That was insane. And gross. Why would I smell it?

I held it in my hand as I walked back to the house. My heart rate was slowing now that I knew no one was chasing me with pitchforks and torches. Though, who knew what tomorrow would hold?

Nancy didn't seem to like Sally, but the rest of the town might. And if they turned on me—

No. I wouldn't think about that.

Penelope jumped through the small dog door before I opened the big door to let myself through. I thumbed the fabric some more and set it on the counter.

I was not going to smell it.

I went through a couple of cabinets, looking for something to eat. But they were completely empty besides cookware and three identical bottles of whiskey, each missing different amounts of amber liquid.

I closed the cabinet. Even if I did drink, this was not the time to lose any of my senses. I half-expected Jake to come knocking on my door to arrest me.

But there was no proof I did anything wrong. I had just gotten here, and as far as I knew, my mere presence didn't kill people.

The piece of fabric on the counter seemed to call me. My brain wanted to smell it so badly.

"It probably just smells like dirt," I said.

Penelope looked up at me like I was losing my mind. Which, maybe I was.

Finally, I gave in and brought the piece of fabric to my nose.

It did not smell like dirt. The smell was different. A bit floral. A bit minty.

Like a rose and a stick of gum had a baby.

What if this was a clue in the investigation?

I glanced outside to the edge of the cornfield where I'd found the piece of fabric. The police likely hadn't gotten that far with their investigation. They'd come out of the cornfield at an angle more towards the front of the house.

Or maybe it was nothing. Just a piece of trash that floated through the breeze and landed in my field.

I put it on the counter again, the smell still lingering in my nostrils and the back of my throat.

I was losing it. I needed sleep.

Penelope snuggled up in a blanket on the third bed we tried, but I couldn't sleep. My mind was going a million miles an hour, and I could not get comfortable.

I needed yoga.

My favorite place in the entire world to do yoga was the top of Mona. One of my boyfriends had created a wood platform, almost like a deck, providing the ground's stability with views of the air. It rested on the front portion of Mona's roof, while the back was reserved for the skylight over the bed.

I unrolled my ratty yoga mat and started my practice. As I moved through each pose, keeping my breath steady, my mind began to clear. The stars were out, and the moon offered a spotlight so bright, I felt like I was on stage.

I didn't know how long I'd been up there, but when I rolled up my mat, I felt at peace. And I knew what I was going to do to clear my name.

I was going to solve the murder.

9

The only problem was, I didn't know how to solve a murder.

The closest to a murder I'd ever been was when a doll I'd gotten from a foster family had its head ripped off by a child of another foster family. I'd seen him do it, so there was no mystery.

And yet, I was the one who ended up going back into the system. Mostly because my hair had turned an angry shade of red and scared the boy out of his wits. Served him right.

Either way, I had no idea what I was doing. I had a boyfriend once—PJ—who loved watching cop shows. I think we watched forty seasons of something to do with dead bodies and finding the murderer. I'd only watched it because I thought he and I might actually end up together. Like forever. But he'd gone and ruined that. Either way, maybe some of those episodes would come in handy. They had to. Because the sooner I cleared my name, the sooner everyone would know I didn't hurt Percy.

That night, sleeping in Mona, I had dreams of being a police officer, uniform and all. I woke up with a fresh sense of purpose.

"Have a great day, Penelope," I said. "I'll buy some food with my tips."

But by the end of the day, I only had twelve dollars and twenty-eight pennies in tips. It seemed the town had turned on me. The farmers wouldn't look me in the eye, and even the two Charlies—who weren't at Helen's when everything happened—acted strangely toward me. Bex was the only one who acted as if nothing was wrong.

When my shift ended, I headed over to the bank. After hearing Sally talk about Percy and Helen's finances so freely, I knew I had to get my paperwork out of there. Heck, she'd probably already read all of it. I sighed. How could I have been so dumb? She obviously hated me from the get-go.

The only thing I could hope for was that Friday was her day off, and I could deal with another teller.

Nope.

She was, once again, the only one there.

"How can I—oh. It's you." She glared. "You have some nerve showing up here."

I sucked in a breath and stood as tall as I could. "I would like to access and close my safe deposit box." I held out the key. "And I'd like a prorated refund."

Sally raised her eyebrows and started laughing.

I didn't know what was so funny but didn't have time to ask before she walked into the backroom.

She emerged, still laughing, with my box.

I inserted the key and pulled the paperwork out. For

what it was worth, it looked like it was in the same position as when I'd put it in.

"That'll be twenty-five dollars," she said, twirling the emerald ring on her right ring finger. She still had on a bunch of jewelry, but her attire was professional.

I held out a hand and waited to collect my money. I didn't know how it could have possibly cost half a year's rent for less than a week, but twenty-five dollars was more than I had and would buy food for at least a few days.

"No," she sneered. "You owe me—the bank—twenty-five dollars."

I could feel my jaw drop.

"You're charging me?"

"It's a hassle fee. I don't know how they do it in big city Colorado, but you can't just open and close accounts willy-nilly around here. It takes up valuable time."

I glanced around at the empty bank. What else would she have been doing? Filing her nails? Trying to pin murders on innocent people? There were no other customers.

"Fine," I said. "I'll keep it open." I closed the box and locked it.

"Sorry," she said. "We don't take empty boxes."

This woman was getting on my last nerve. "Fine." I unlocked and reopened the box. "Does this work?"

I retrieved the change from my pocket and let each and every one of the twenty-eight pennies drop one-by-one into the metal box.

Clink. Clink. Clink, clink, clink. Every time one dropped, Sally flinched.

When they were all in there, I closed the box, locked it, and handed it back to her, shaking it for effect.

Her face was bright red. If she had magical hair, it would have probably exploded by now.

"Take good care of it for me," I said and turned to walk out.

"You know, people must really hate you to give you that many pennies as tips."

Her comment made me hesitate. I'd never heard of this phenomenon.

"A penny is worse than no tip at all."

I reached for the door and pushed until I was in the fresh air again.

I got behind Mona's wheel and cleared my throat to keep the tears back. I'd need another yoga session. But first, I needed food.

***

The small-town market had exactly what I needed—milk, cereal, peanut butter, and popcorn. Which was all I could afford with the twelve dollars I had.

I was walking back to Mona when a shiny silver pickup pulled up next to me. When Earl gingerly stepped out, I thought he was going to yell at me. Or accuse me of killing Percy.

Instead, he pointed at my van. "Do you really do what that says?"

I glanced over at the words I'd painted—Relief with Ellie.

"Yes," I said.

Earl looked to his left and right, making sure no one was around. "I need your help. My back is all out of whack."

Giddiness rose inside me, replacing the frustration of the day.

"If you can fix me, I'll make it worth your while," he said.

I nodded.

"Come to my house tonight around eight. The wife will be out with her friends."

I nodded again, feeling like one of those little plastic bobblehead dogs.

"Good," he said in his deep voice and walked away without another word.

I waited until I was inside Mona to do my happy dance.

My first client!

Penelope loved her peanut butter and popcorn dinner. I had two bowls of cereal before I double-checked—for the fifth time since I'd gotten home—that I had everything I'd need to help Earl. I'd taken the paperwork up to Esme's room and hidden it behind a row of books on the bookshelf. A few titles caught my eye, like one about premonitions, but I didn't have the attention span to sit down and read a book. I was too excited about working with Earl.

I didn't want to be early, in case his wife hadn't left yet. When it was about twenty minutes 'til eight, I made my way very slowly toward his house. His property was on the other side of Percy and Helen's.

"You're almost late," Earl said, meeting me on his porch. His house was made of logs—similar to what you might find in the mountains—but the giant silver cylindrical silos behind it were a dead giveaway that we were still in Iowa.

"I didn't want to run into your wife," I said. It was only slightly awkward that I was sneaking around with a man almost three times my age behind his wife's back. Okay, maybe more than slightly.

"Katie left an hour ago," he said.

"Katie?" I asked, feeling my stomach sour. "As in my boss, Katie?"

"Technically, Bex's your boss. But yes, Katie of Katie's Café."

I almost backed out right then and there. My job at Katie's was the only way I was even slightly surviving, and if I couldn't help Earl, he wouldn't pay me, and I could lose my job there too.

"Don't worry." Earl waved for me to come inside. "Let's get this show on the road."

I grabbed the stretching sheet I'd prepared along with a couple of exercise bands and a yoga mat.

His home decor was that of an artist's. Large paintings hung on tall walls that reached up to a vaulted ceiling. Huge windows looked out past the silos and into the field.

"First, can you tell me what kind of pain you're experiencing and where it's located?"

Earl huffed. "It's my back. It hurt before, but ever since the fight, it's been almost unbearable."

"Do you think something could be broken?" I asked.

He shook his head. "I went to the doctor—Katie made me. Everything checked out. They gave me pain meds, but I'm not going to get addicted like some Hollywood flunky."

"Let's start with a baseline range of motion test, okay?" I explained how I was going to measure his movements so we could keep up with his progress. "Now, can you bend forward and touch your toes?"

He winced but did, though his fingertips only reached as far as his knees.

"Good," I said. "Now turn to each side."

Once I had all the measurements, we started with the stretches I'd outlined on the sheet. Earl gritted his teeth through most of it but never made a peep. He was a tough old guy.

"You're doing great," I said as we reached the final stretch.

"You don't have to cheer me on," Earl grumbled under his breath. But I'd noticed every time I gave him positive feedback, he seemed to work just a bit harder.

"For the last stretch, we're going to try downward dog," I said. "It's a yoga pose—"

"Where I put my butt in the air?" He laughed. "My daughter used to do it all the time."

Ah, so he had a daughter. "Do you have any other children?"

"Just the one."

Once he was in the position, I asked, "Do you mind if I push on your lower back?"

"Go ahead."

I eased him deeper into the stretch, gently letting my palms rest on his back. "How is that?"

"Fine," he said. "My daughter's too good for Iowa. Ran off to be an actress."

In college, they taught us to make conversation with the clients to take their mind off the pain of the stretch, but until now, Earl had been completely shut off.

"Has she been in anything I might have seen?"

"I don't watch TV," he said. "Don't have time managing a farm. But she's in some TV show about superheroes."

"The one with the tiger woman?"

"That's the one," he said. "She's the tiger woman."

That explained the conversation he had with Hank my first morning at the café.

"You must be proud."

"I'd be proud if she'd run this farm like we have for generations. TV is for the lazy. I didn't raise her to be lazy."

I almost mentioned that it wasn't like she was sitting around watching TV. She was acting. Which was probably pretty tough.

"I can't believe he's dead," Earl said, changing the subject.

"Were you close?" I pushed a little harder. "Only a few more seconds in the stretch."

"No, we weren't close," Earl grumbled. "Everyone adored him, but I could see right through his act. He was a pain in my butt. Always coming onto my property with his tractors and that stupid chopping blade. He didn't know how to harvest a field properly. I didn't want him anywhere near my corn."

"So, you fought?" I eased up, letting him rest.

"All the time." Earl was loosening up as the seconds ticked by. "That day at Fran's Feed, I punched him before he knocked me over a stack of concrete bags. Fran was so angry with us."

"Do you think someone killed him?" I asked hesitantly, unsure whether he would accuse me.

"Course I do," Earl said. "Probably Helen after she found out about—"

I removed my hands, and Earl came to a stand without finishing his sentence.

"After she found out about what?" I asked. I assumed it was about him emptying their bank account, but I didn't want to spread rumors if that's not what he was talking about.

"Nothing," he said. "I shouldn't spread rumors. I'm always getting on Katie about town gossip, and here I am going on about other people's business with the new girl."

To say I was disappointed would be an understatement, but I couldn't push. Especially if I wanted to keep him as a long-term client.

"How do you feel now?"

Earl twisted from side to side, gently at first, then with more vigor. "I think you've healed me," he said, his eyes wide.

"I'm not sure you should overdo it. You're feeling limber now, but you'll probably be sore tomorrow."

"Wait here." He left the room. I used the chance to

clean up the equipment we'd used and scribble down some notes on how it went.

When he came back, he pushed a wad of cash into my hand.

"Whoa," I said, looking down at the bills. "This is way too much."

"I've never felt this good in my life," he said. "If I had more cash, I'd give it to you. I didn't get any out of the Shazam. I thought betting on you would be like betting on a three-legged-racehorse."

"The Shazam?" It sounded like a genie in a bottle or something.

"You know, at the bank?" He frowned. "A—uh—an ATM."

"I've never heard an ATM called a Shazam." I laughed. "Let's do the final range of motion test so we know where to go from here."

"Where to go? There's nowhere to go." He bent over and touched the ground. "See? I've never been able to do that."

I gaped at him. Had he been messing with me before when he could only touch his knees? During my internship, I'd seen people get better, but it was usually after several sessions.

He stood and put his arms out to the side. "Ta-da."

"Okay, then," I said. "I suppose my work here is done."

"I'm no businessman, but maybe you shouldn't do such good work."

"What do you mean?"

"If you heal everyone on the first go-round, you won't have any repeat customers."

"I'll keep that in mind." Not that I had any way of controlling how well someone would react to the exercises.

"I'll tell everyone in town you're not a murderer." Earl opened the door for me. "Not that they'll listen to me, but I can try."

My heart felt like it dropped into my stomach. I'd almost forgotten about the murder drama.

"Here's a sheet of the stretches we did today." I handed him the sheet I'd created. "You should do these at least once or twice a day to keep your back limber. Drink lots of water tonight and tomorrow. And if the pain comes back, let me know."

He took the sheet and thanked me as I walked out, still holding the wad of cash.

Overall, it was a successful first job. I earned some money, and though he may not have told me anything substantial about Percy's case, I now knew where to start: with Helen.

10

The next morning at the café, I was renewed with energy. I'd done my moonlight yoga the night before and counted the money Earl had given me—almost a hundred dollars.

Earl didn't let on that he and I were on good terms when I poured his coffee, but knowing he was on my side made me feel better. The empty chair at their table was almost like a memorial for Percy. No one sat in it the day before, and no one sat in it today.

Until Ty walked in and sat down like it was no big deal.

All four men—Earl, Hank, William, and George—looked like they wanted to say something, but Ty seemed completely oblivious. "I'll take a coffee," he said to me with a smile.

Okay, maybe he was on my side too.

I poured the coffee and said. "Thanks for getting the harvesting done. The field is so much bigger than I thought. It would have been impossible for me to get through it all."

"It was no big deal," Ty said. "Once the police clear the scene, I'll finish up the last square. Do you know if they found anything out there?"

I shook my head. "They come and go, but no one tells me anything."

"I heard he died of internal injuries," Hank said, not looking in Earl's direction.

Earl didn't even glance up from his paper.

"Deb told Sally his face was completely black and blue," Ty said. "And that he had abrasions all over his body."

While Hank didn't look at Earl, Ty was staring him down.

Earl calmly folded his paper and looked up at Ty. "Is there something you'd like to ask me, young man?"

Ty puffed his chest and asked, "Did you kill my uncle?"

Earl took a sip of his coffee. "First, your girlfriend accuses Ellie, and now you're accusing me? Seems like you're grasping at straws. Percy was known to enjoy his rum. He probably tied one on, stumbled his way over to the Vanderwick farm, and keeled over."

"He wasn't drinking that night," Ty said. "I was with him for dinner. He had tea."

"Then you probably noticed he wasn't black and blue," Earl said. "We got in a tussle, but I only got one good swing in before he knocked me over those concrete bags and messed up my back."

"Speaking of backs," William said, pushing his glasses up the bridge of his nose. "You seem to feel better."

"Much," Earl said, standing. He tucked the paper

under his arm and threw a twenty down. "Coffee's on me."

I acted as if I hadn't heard everything that had just happened, but when Earl passed, he whispered, "Thanks again."

I poured some coffee for a couple of teenagers in a corner booth, then made my way back over to the group of men to refill their coffee.

"For what it's worth," Ty said to me. "We don't think you had anything to do with Percy's death."

"Speak for yourself," William said. "There wasn't an ounce of crime in this town before she showed up. It reminds me of when Esme's family came to town."

"Esme was a good woman," Ty said, his face turning bright red. "You don't get to speak about her that way."

"I mean no disrespect," William continued. "I'm simply stating the obvious. The Vanderwick women know how to wreak havoc in Cliff Haven."

I gritted my teeth against the emotion that was slowly climbing to my scalp. They could say what they wanted. I would prove them wrong.

"Ellie did not kill Percy," a man said from behind me. I turned to see Jake and Deb in their uniforms with frowns on their faces.

"Can I get you some coffee?" I asked as Bex had instructed on my first day.

"Yes, please." Jake took a seat at one of the four-person square tables. Deb sat across from him.

"Do you know who did?" Hank asked.

Jake shrugged. "Maybe no one. We still haven't ruled

out the possibility that it was an accident or that he died of natural causes."

"Internal bleeding isn't usually a natural cause," Ty said.

"The rumor about internal bleeding is just that," Deb said. "So we can just put that one to bed right now."

"Did you or did you not tell Sally that Percy was black and blue?" Ty said.

Deb's face paled as Jake turned his attention on her.

"What I say to Sally should stay between the two of us," Deb said. "I guess you've rubbed off on her."

"What's that supposed to mean?" Ty looked like he was ready for a fight.

"It means I won't tell Sally any more secrets," Deb muttered.

"Can I—uh—get you something to eat?" I asked as I poured a coffee for each of them.

"I'll take a big stack of pancakes," Jake said. "And make sure they keep the crunchy bits attached. Sometimes Big Charlie cuts them off."

I nearly dropped my pen. He liked the crunchy bits too?

"I'll do a ham and cheese omelet," Deb said. "With hash browns."

I wrote both orders down and made my way to the kitchen. First, we had the same eyes, and now we both like the crunchy bits on the pancakes?

I shook my head.

No.

I couldn't let myself get wrapped up in this. He wasn't

my father. Everyone probably liked the crunchy bits. It wasn't like food preferences were hereditary, right?

Plus, I needed to focus on the investigation.

When I walked back out into the dining area, Ty was stomping out the front door.

"What happened?" I asked.

No one answered. No one even met my eye.

The entire room paused. No one moved. No one talked.

It wasn't until the most dazzling woman I'd seen in Cliff Haven walked through the door that everything seemed to resume. She wore sleek black pants, a white blouse, and a gray and black animal print blazer that shimmered ever so slightly. Her hair was a sleek light gray, and her lipstick was the color of a deep red wine. But the best part was her shoes—pristine silver glitter and white tennis shoes.

She walked right over to me and stopped with her hands on her hips.

"Can I get you any coffee?" I asked. "Or a menu?"

"Are you the woman who was sneaking around with my husband last night?"

My stomach dropped.

Katie.

"I wasn't—I didn't—nothing happened," I stammered.

Everyone was looking at us.

I could feel my hair start to twist into curls. Thankfully, it was in a ponytail.

"Something happened all right," she said.

"I just helped him stretch out his back."

Bex and Deb gasped at the same time.

"Not like that," I said. I reached up and twisted my ponytail into a bun, tucking the ends in so no one would notice the curling. Now, I only had to hope it wouldn't change color. "I have a business. I'm a licensed recreational therapist. I help people with their body, mind, and soul issues."

Before I could say anything else, her face turned up into a smile, and she wrapped me in a hug tighter than a new sports bra. She smelled like exotic spices.

"Thank you so much," she whispered in my ear.

I didn't know what to do. I just patted her on the back until she let go.

"He's like a brand-new man," she said. "Do you think you could look at my shoulders? I'd love to improve my range of motion."

She lifted her arms to shoulder height. "That's all the further they go anymore."

"I—uh—I think we could work on that," I said, my heart rate returning to normal.

"Wait, hold on," Hank said. "Are you saying she's a healer or something?"

"No." I shook my head. "No, no, no. I'm not a healer."

"But you healed Earl's back?" William asked.

"I helped him work out some tension, that's all." I didn't want to oversell my services. "His results are not typical results."

"You're just being modest," Katie said. "How about you come over tonight? I'm having all the girls over for dessert."

I hesitated. Katie might have wanted me there, but the

other women probably didn't. Especially Helen, if she thought I killed her husband.

"I'll make it worth your while," Katie said. "Please."

"Okay," I finally answered. "I'll be there."

Katie clapped her hands together in triumph.

Before I went home to get ready to meet with the women, I headed over to Fran's Feed and Fabric. I'd never heard of a feed store mixed with a fabric store, but somehow when I walked in, it worked. The feed was in one section, and the fabric was toward the back of the store in its own section.

"It's about time you showed up," a woman said from behind the counter. "I thought you might never come in."

I didn't know why she had expected me to show up, but she seemed friendly enough. She had long white hair that stuck out all over the place. Her skin was tanned to the point of being leathery, and she wore no discernable makeup. But the smile on her face was stunning.

"I'm Fran." She shook my hand with a tight grip. "I'm guessing you're here to get some food for the sweet little piglet I keep hearing about."

Ah, so that's why she would have expected me.

"Yes," I said. "And I wanted to know about the argument between Earl and Percy the other day."

She laughed. "You get right to the point, don't ya?"

I shrugged. "I guess so."

"I like that. Esme was like that too." She pulled a bag of feed with a pig on the front down from a shelf. "I bet you want to know all about her, don't you?"

I nodded. "But no one seems to want to talk about her."

"They're still grieving," she said. "When a woman like Esme dies, it's like a black hole opens and gobbles up everything in its path. The pain is still too fresh."

"But Esme knew she was going to die, right? Didn't that give everyone a chance to come to terms with it?"

"You can try to come to terms with death, but until it happens, there's only so much you can do."

"What about you? Are you grieving her death?"

"In my own way," Fran said. "Esme and I weren't the closest. We had a bit of a rivalry. But I still loved her all the same."

"Did you know my mother?"

"Didn't you want to talk about that fight?" Fran asked, completely changing the subject.

I sighed. "Can you tell me about it?"

"Why?" She gave me a suspicious look.

"I just—"

"Feel like you need to solve it to clear your name?"

Wow. Word traveled fast in small towns.

"For one, yes, I'd like to clear my name," I answered, standing up as straight as I could. "And I also feel partially responsible, even though I didn't do it. He was found on Esme's—my—property after all."

"I heard you thought the corn killed him." She doubled over in a fit of laughter.

I was getting nowhere with this woman. "How much do I owe you for the pig feed?"

"Oh, come on now, it's funny. I bet it tasted awful."

It did, but I wouldn't give her the satisfaction of agreeing with her. It was no wonder she and Esme weren't close.

I pulled out some cash I'd gotten from Earl. Tips were still pretty slow, even though it was a Saturday and we were crazy busy. But I'd only gotten thirteen pennies today, so that was a plus.

"Will twenty do it?" I set two tens on the counter.

"Okay, all right." She caught her breath. "I'll tell you about the fight."

She punched in a couple of numbers on the register and made change from one of the tens. "Percy and Earl were always fighting. They couldn't agree on the color of the sky. But this fight was different," she said. "This fight was about something Percy was keeping secret. Earl didn't like it, so he punched Percy, and Percy pushed him over those concrete bags right over there." She pointed to a pile of concrete bags that were neatly stacked. "They were a bugger to clean up. My back is still feeling it."

"Do you know what Percy was keeping secret?"

"Sounded like something about money. Maybe he owed Earl money or something."

"What happened after the fight?" I asked. "Do you think that was the end of it?"

"Who knows," Fran said. "I heard Percy had internal bleeding and was pretty beat up."

"I think that's just a rumor," I said. "Deb said they don't know for sure how he died."

"Might not have been how he died, but it still could have been true."

That was a thought.

"Thank you for the insight," I said. "And for the pig feed. Penelope will be very excited."

As I was walking out the door, I heard her say, "A pet pig. Who would have thought?"

When I got home, I checked the mailbox for the first time. I'd completely forgotten, and it showed. The box was packed.

I began opening bill after bill. According to the paperwork Esme sent, the house was paid for, but the electricity was overdue, as were the propane, the trash pickup, and the water and sewer.

Houses were expensive.

I thought I'd struck it rich when Earl paid me. But I was a couple hundred dollars short of paying the bills. And that was just for this month.

I plopped down on the sofa and sighed. Penelope nudged me to pick her up. She snuggled into me like she always did when she could tell I was upset. "I'll just have to work extra hard tonight to get the women to trust me. Then they'll spread the word, and my business will take off."

I arrived early with all the resources I could find. Since Katie hadn't given me any indication of what I would do, I needed to be prepared for anything.

"You made it," Katie said, greeting me with a warm hug. She wore paint-spattered yoga pants, a black tank, and an oversized purple wrap with long sleeves. "Come on in."

I walked to the back of the house—further than I'd been with Earl—where a bunch of women sat around a large table. The dining room had easels with paintings in various stages of completion pushed into the corners.

The women sipped from coffee mugs and chatted while thumbing through magazines. The minute they saw me, they went silent.

"Come on now, ladies," Katie said. "Won't you help me make Ellie feel welcome?"

One of the ladies with mousy brown hair and pursed lips stood and walked past us. "I won't be in the company of a murderer," she hissed.

Katie shrugged. "Anyone else?"

Two more women—a mother and a daughter, it seemed—stood and left, though they were a bit nicer about it. "I think it's best we go too," the mother said.

"Have a seat," Katie said, directing me to an empty chair next to a woman who had been at Helen's. The one with the blue, dyed hair. "This is Amy."

"Hello," I said, sitting down. The only women left were Amy, Fran, and Katie.

"Would you like something to drink?" Katie asked, acting as if nothing had happened. "I have tea and coffee —regular or decaf."

It felt strange for someone to wait on me. "Decaf would be fine."

"Cream or sugar?"

"No, thank you."

"I hear you healed Earl," Amy said, her voice coarse like she'd been smoking since she was a teenager. She wore a pair of stained gray sweatpants and a sleeveless t-shirt with a metal band on the front.

"I wouldn't say I healed him," I said. "I just helped him work out some muscle tension."

"She healed him," Katie said, setting the coffee down in front of me. "It's like night and day. He's so much happier."

"Why wouldn't he be?" Amy said. "He probably feels like a new man."

"He sure acted like it last night." Katie winked, and the other two women laughed. The back of my neck probably turned the color of a lobster.

"Did you hear about Percy?" Amy asked Katie.

"What about him?" Helen said from the doorway. Her face was completely flushed, and she seemed out of breath. She had on running shoes, black running tights, and an oversized sweatshirt with a tractor on the front.

Amy didn't even look abashed that we were talking about Helen's dead husband behind her back. "I heard someone poisoned him."

"Who told you that?" Katie asked, handing Helen a steaming cup of coffee.

Helen stayed standing as if she might dart for the door at any moment. When our gazes met, she glared at me.

"Just overheard someone talking about it at the shop today." Amy avoided Helen's gaze. "Doesn't matter who."

"First, he was beaten to death, now poison?" Helen scoffed. "No one knows what they're talking about."

The wheels in my mind turned. Was Helen brushing the idea to the side because she'd poisoned him? She *had* mentioned she had poison in her house for the mice. What if she used it to kill her husband?

"We should probably keep the gossip to a minimum until we get the official police report," Katie said. Apparently, Earl telling her not to gossip was working.

"The police aren't talking," Helen said. "I think they think I killed him."

Then we were all on the same page.

Katie laughed. "That's absurd. We know you wouldn't kill Percy. You were the perfect couple."

Helen rolled her eyes so far back in her head, she lost her balance and almost tipped over.

"Did you run here?" Katie asked.

"I couldn't run if I tried," Helen said. "My hips are all messed up."

I would guess Helen had one too many glasses of wine, but I wasn't about to give my opinion.

Fran scowled. "Was there trouble in paradise?"

These women talked to each other like they were sisters, not just friends. I guess that's how small towns worked. And if they did, these women probably knew just about everything about Esme.

"No one is perfect," Helen said. "Not one single person. Not me. Definitely not Percy." She hiccupped.

I kept my gaze in my cup. Somehow, I needed to figure out what Helen knew.

"Okay, that's enough of that," Katie said. "I invited Ellie to join us tonight. If you haven't already heard, Ellie worked wonders on Earl's back, and I wanted to see if she could help us too. Of course, I told her we'd pay her handsomely for her services."

Amy and Fran nodded. Helen leaned against the wall and sipped her coffee.

"Why don't we go through each of your ailments." I'd never done a group therapy session before, but it would make the night go more smoothly if I could do some exercises to hit all their problems.

Amy started, "My lower back is killing me from moving around all those antiques. But I have to keep the store fresh. Otherwise, why would people come in?"

"Your store is a gem," Katie said, then turned her attention to me. "People come from all around to visit."

Amy blushed.

"My hands and wrists are the worst." Fran rotated her hands in circles, a flash of pain crossing her face. "But my back is bad too from moving those concrete bags."

"I'm awful sorry about that," Katie said. "I don't know what got into Earl that day."

"It wasn't Earl's fault," Helen said. "If Percy were alive, I'd tell him to apologize to Fran and Earl."

We all gaped at her, but she offered no more information.

"I needed the exercise," Fran said. "It wasn't such a big deal."

"As I told you this morning," Katie said. "My range of motion in my shoulders is horrible."

I nodded and took down a few notes. I glanced up at Helen, waiting for her to tell me her problem.

"Go on, Helen, she can help you," Katie said.

Helen's eyes glossed over with tears—the first sign of sadness she'd shown since she arrived. "It's just, I don't have any money to pay you with."

"What do you mean you don't have any money?" Katie asked.

Helen didn't answer. She just shook her head and looked out the dark window.

"It's really okay. I'd like to help if I can," I said. "You said your hips are bothering you?"

She let out a tiny laugh. "If you can fix my hips, you'll do what no doctor or physical therapist has been able to do short of giving me crazy amounts of pain meds."

"I'll see what I can do," I said. "Our best bet is to start with some general stretching."

12

We walked into the living room where Katie had pushed all the furniture out of the way. We started with deep breathing exercises moving their arms up and down, their necks all around. Then we moved down their bodies, all the way to their toes.

As they did each stretch, I took notes about the opportunities I saw for each of them. Then I gave each of them specific exercises to work on for their individual problems. While Amy and Helen stretched, I helped move Fran's wrists and Katie's arms slightly further than their original positions. After about thirty minutes, I began the cooldown.

"How does that feel?" I asked as each of the women came to a stand.

"My pain is completely gone," Fran said, moving her wrists around. "That's amazing."

"Mine's still there, but it feels slightly better," Amy said, her tone unsure.

"Sometimes—most times—it takes several sessions to work out the kinks, and then it takes continued exercise to keep everything loose and strong." I handed each of them the exercise sheets I thought they could use. "These are simple fifteen-minute exercises you can do once or twice a day to stay limber."

"Thank you so much," Katie said, taking her sheet. "This means the world to us."

Helen was the last to approach me. "I guess I shouldn't have been surprised that this did absolutely nothing for me."

I'd noticed an improvement in her range of motion when she was doing the butterfly stretch, but I wasn't about to contradict her.

"I'd be happy to work with you a bit more," I said. "No charge."

The other women had gone back to their activities and chatter at the table.

"First, I have to know." She crossed her arms over her chest. "Did you kill Percy? Not that I'll be mad, and I won't tell anyone, but I need to know." She was so close I could smell the alcohol on her breath. Was she asking to keep me from suspecting she did it?

"I swear to you, I did not kill Percy."

I thought I heard her mumble, "too bad," under her breath.

"Why don't you sit on a chair and lean forward," I said. "Do you mind if I put my hands on your upper back?"

She shook her head and pulled her hair up.

I gently pushed her forward, her body hinge at the hips. "How does that feel?"

"It doesn't hurt if that's what you're asking."

No pain was good. "Okay, now let's go back to that butterfly position." I sat on the floor with the soles of my feet together. She did the same, the tips of our toes touching. "Now, I want you to reach forward and grab my hands."

She did, and I gently pulled so she was hinging forward. "Just tell me if it hurts."

"It's fine," she mumbled.

I was counting in my head when she started talking. At first, it sounded like she was talking to me, but then it seemed like maybe she was just talking to herself.

"Percy was no good from the start. I should have listened to my mama. I should have never trusted such a smooth-talker. I should have signed the prenup. Why would he have been interested in me? I was a nerd. He could have had any girl in the school. It was because he knew I wouldn't do anything to go against him. He knew I'd be a pushover. He knew I'd never leave him."

"I heard he had some problems with money."

She looked at me in shock as if she'd forgotten I was there.

"Sorry," I said. "It's none of my business." I pulled a bit harder, stretching her farther forward.

"Percy kept track of everything. Every single dime. He told me a hundred times we were just getting by. That we could hardly afford the food on the table." She sighed.

I was confused. "But the farm and the hardware store?"

"It turns out we were doing better than I knew. He was just giving it all away."

"What do you mean?" I asked.

Helen hesitated. "Please don't tell the others."

I shook my head. "I won't." I couldn't believe she was so open with me, but she was tipsy, so maybe that had something to do with it.

"He gave it to his son."

"His son?" I asked. "But I thought—"

"Not *my* son," she clarified. "His son. With another woman."

She let go of my hands, sat back up, and started crying.

I scooched around to sit next to her and rubbed her back, trying to comfort her.

"He told me a week ago," she said. "He had given this boy everything. I don't know what was worse—the fact that we couldn't have a child, but he did with someone else, or that he'd given that child everything. They went on trips. Together. As a family. I looked up the boy's social media."

"That must have been so hard." I couldn't imagine being married that long only to find out I'd been completely duped.

"But the worst part was, he wanted to give him the farm. My farm," she said. "He wanted me to sign off on it. Told me if I didn't, he'd leave me."

"But if you got divorced, at least you'd get half the farm, right?" I asked.

"Probably," she said. "But he would have gotten half of the hardware store too. And then everyone would know we didn't have the fairytale life they all thought we did."

I felt horrible for her, but she really wasn't making herself look less guilty. All of this sounded like the perfect motive to kill someone.

"And now I can't even pay my bills. I'm going to lose the farm anyway if I don't find some money soon."

"I'm so sorry."

Helen stood and then looked down at me, horrified. "I can't believe I just told you all of that." She walked to the door and pulled her coat off the hanger. "If you tell anyone, I'll deny it. You'll sound crazy."

Before I could assure her I wouldn't tell anyone, she was gone.

I walked back into the dining area, and Katie said, "Did you help Helen?"

"Uh, I don't know," I said. "She had to leave in a hurry. Maybe someone should go offer her a ride."

Fran and Amy exchanged looks. "We should go too," they said. "We can take her home on our way."

They stood and gathered their belongings.

"Thank you for your help," Fran said. "I think Amy wants to schedule a follow-up."

"Absolutely," I said. "I work at the diner most mornings, but afternoons and evenings are free for me."

"I'll let you know," Amy said.

Katie waited until it was just the two of us before handing me a pile of cash. "I hope this covers Helen's too."

And just like that, my bills would be paid.

13

Well, most of my bills.

When I did the final tally, I realized I was still about fifty dollars short. Which meant no more groceries.

Oh well, Penelope had pig food, and I had cereal. We'd lived on less.

Percy's funeral was after work on Monday. I wore my nicest black pants. Okay, they were yoga pants, but they didn't look like it when I paired them with ballet flats and the only blouse I owned. Which had flowers on it. But at least it wasn't a tank top.

Note to self: buy clothes when I had more money.

Helen stood at the door of the town church, greeting everyone with tears in her eyes.

When I approached, she acted like she was talking to someone else, completely ignoring me.

Katie waved me over to join her and Earl.

"You made it," Katie said. "I know you didn't know

Percy, but I'm sure it means an awful lot to Helen that you're here."

If it did, Helen had a strange way of showing it.

"It seemed like the right thing to do," I said. "How's your back?" I asked Earl.

"It's as good as the day I graduated high school. Better, actually."

"And your shoulders?" I asked Katie.

"They feel great," she said, lifting her arms straight in the air, showing off her toned midriff.

Earl pulled her shirt down playfully and then kissed her on the cheek.

Katie leaned toward me to whisper, "I know Earl already told you this, but you shouldn't do such a good job. If you left us in a bit of pain, you'd have recurring customers."

"If only I had control over that," I said. "It seems you all are quick healers."

"We're not the healers, my dear." Katie winked. "I think the service is about to begin."

"I need to use the restroom," I said. "Do you know where it is?"

"Do I know where it is?" She laughed. "I've gone to church here since the Sunday after I was born. It's down the hall to the left. We'll save you a seat by us."

The bathroom was exactly where she said it would be. I checked to make sure my hair was behaving in its high bun. It was still smooth and white.

I was almost back to the sanctuary when I heard someone whispering around the corner.

"I tried," the voice said. "I had the key, but it wouldn't turn in the lock."

I wanted to peek around the corner to see who was talking but stayed back.

"They're gone now." The voice paused. "Don't get caught."

I waited a few moments, but the conversation seemed to be over. When I came around the corner, there was no one there.

Whatever the person was talking about, it sounded illegal.

But it wasn't my business.

I joined Earl and Katie on the right side of the small church and tried to keep my emotions in check while the funeral proceeded. I hated funerals. I hated being sad.

Dozens of people stood to talk about how Percy had changed their lives. How his simple presence in the community changed it into what it was today. Helen even lied her way through a sweet speech.

When it was over, we had the option to walk out past the casket and see Percy or go straight outside. I wanted to leave, but I thought maybe if I got a closer look at Percy's face, it would give me some clue as to who did this. And whether that was Helen.

Percy looked waxy and not at all beaten up. His hands lay folded on his stomach, and he wore a nice suit. Nothing on him gave away any clues.

"He wore that for our wedding," Helen said, coming up next to me. "The first and only time I saw him in a suit. It looks strange on him."

We both looked down into the casket as people around us congregated.

"I'm sorry I was rude earlier," Helen whispered. "I should never have spoken of my personal problems. But you're very easy to talk to."

I'd been told that my entire life.

And I'd learned to keep people's secrets after I'd revealed to one of my foster mothers that my foster father was secretly seeing one of my teachers.

They'd split up. I ended up back in the system.

"Don't worry," I said. "I promise I won't say anything to anyone. Your private business is yours alone."

"Here's Helen," Amy said, approaching us with a man I'd thought I'd never see again. "Helen, this man says he needs to speak with you."

If the man needed to talk to Helen, he was doing a terrible job of it. Instead, he gaped at me, fear written all over his face.

The last time I'd seen him, he had the same expression. Likely because my hair had twisted itself into braids and turned bright green.

"What are you doing here?" Helen asked, bringing his attention back to her.

"Uh—I—wanted to see my father," PJ said.

"Well, go right ahead," Helen stepped to the side and motioned toward Percy.

Amy and Katie gasped.

PJ took a step away from the casket rather than toward it. For him to get to it, he would have to go past me.

"What's your problem?" Helen asked. "Came all this way from Chicago only to freeze up at the sight of him?"

PJ wore expensive jeans and a fancy western button-down shirt. His bedazzled boots and perfectly clean cowboy hat completed the hipster cowboy look. When he lived in Denver, he always wore hoodies and loose-fitting jeans. I'd almost think he was a different person if he wasn't gaping at me.

"She—" PJ pointed at me, terror written all over his face.

"Ellie?" Helen asked. "What does Ellie have to do with this?"

But PJ didn't respond. Instead, he passed out right there in the aisle of the church.

14

Helen kicked at his boot. "He's out cold."

"Was he implying Percy is his father?" Amy asked.

Helen sighed. "Percy is his father. Or was, I suppose." She threw a glance back at Percy, who still lay serenely in the coffin. If he could somehow see what was transpiring, would he have been ashamed?

"I didn't think you knew," Earl said.

"You knew?" Katie and Helen both said at the same time.

I glanced down at PJ. He might have looked terrified, but fear was working its way up my spine too. PJ knew about my hair. What if he told everyone? People already hated me because they thought I killed Percy. If they found out I had some weird color-changing hair, they'd surely run me out of town before I'd ever learned about my history.

"Ellie?" PJ's voice was soft as his eyelashes fluttered awake.

All eyes turned toward me.

"You know him?" Helen asked, her face accusatory.

"Yes," I said. "I mean, I didn't know he was Percy's son," I added quickly. "But I dated him around a year ago when I lived in Colorado."

"You dated him?" Katie asked. "You dated Percy's illegitimate son?" Hopefully, the shocked look on her face was because she was still trying to process the fact that Percy had a son, not because she was mad that I dated PJ.

"I am not illegitimate," PJ said, sitting up. "Percy was my father. I was named after him. He and my mother were together thirty years. They had me twenty-eight years ago."

Helen looked down at her shoes.

"And you knew about this?" Katie asked Helen.

"I only found out a few days ago," Helen said, her voice thick with emotion. "I had no idea Percy had been living a double life nearly our entire marriage."

I took a step back behind Earl. PJ could forget I existed for all I cared, but I couldn't leave. I needed to find out what was going on in case it had something to do with Percy's death.

"Maybe we should all go outside and discuss this in the fresh air," Amy said.

"I think we should discuss this right here." PJ stood to his feet and walked to the casket, not looking at me. "This man was my father, and he left me everything. I'm just here to take what's mine."

"What exactly do you think is yours?" Ty said from the back of the church. He wasn't wearing nice clothes. Not what you'd expect someone to wear at their uncle's funeral. It looked like he was wearing work clothes. Mud caked his boots, and there were holes in his jeans.

"The farm, the rest of the money." PJ shrugged.

"The *rest* of the money?" Helen said.

"The income from the farm." PJ pulled out a piece of paper and handed it to Helen. "This is Percy's will. It says I inherit everything."

Ty glanced over Helen's shoulder as she examined the paperwork.

"I'm sorry to say, young man," Hank said, coming down the aisle. "You cannot inherit what did not legally belong to Percy. The farm has been in my family for ages, and I believe Helen signed a prenuptial agreement that said Percy was entitled to none of it."

"And the money Percy has been sending you was my money," Helen said. "And I'd appreciate it if you'd give it back."

"There's nothing to give back," PJ said.

"What do you mean, there's nothing to give back?" Helen said.

When we dated, PJ drove a fancy car and always took me to expensive restaurants. It almost made me feel guilty for indirectly using Helen's money.

"You have to spend money to make money," PJ continued. "My mother and I have a lifestyle we've come to expect. And Percy made it very clear he would take care of us even more so after his death. Which means I'll acquire the property and develop it."

I raised an eyebrow. It sounded like motive for murder.

"We'll just get an attorney on the phone," Hank said.

"I don't have money for an attorney," Helen said. "Percy gave it all to him."

PJ didn't even have the decency to look ashamed. Though, it wasn't his fault his father was a loser who stole from one family to give to another.

"I'll cover the attorney," Hank said. "We won't let this boy get our farm."

"No way," Ty said. "The only one getting that farm when you die is me."

Hank glared over at his son.

"What? It's true," he said. "I'm the rightful heir. I've worked those farms since I was a toddler."

"This is not the time to discuss who will get what," Hank growled. "I believe we have a reception to go to."

Helen nodded.

"You're welcome to come," Hank said to PJ. "So long as you can behave yourself."

PJ took one last look in the casket then asked. "Will there be food?"

Helen looked like she might slap him, but Ty got there first.

He tackled PJ to the floor, yelling obscenities.

Hank and Earl got Ty off PJ, but Ty was not done calling him every name in the book.

"That is enough," Hank bellowed. "You two. My truck. Now."

Ty and PJ followed Hank from the church.

I helped Helen outside. "Do you need a ride home?"

"That would be wonderful," Helen said. "I came with Hank, but I don't want to be anywhere near PJ."

We walked out to Mona in silence. Helen and I were

both lost in thought. Initially, I thought it looked like Helen might have offed Percy. And I don't know that I would have blamed her . . . much. Okay, I know murder is wrong. But to be betrayed like that. Used like that. It would be hard not to want to do something about it.

But maybe PJ did it. He never seemed like the violent type, but he was obsessed with those crime shows. He could have taken some pointers to get what he wanted when he found out Helen wouldn't sign away the farm.

As we rumbled down the road, I turned to Helen. "You don't have to tell me anything, but I wanted to ask. When Percy asked you to sign away the farm, you said no, right?"

"Right," Helen said. "I was beside myself. I had just found out he had a son. And then he wants me to give up my home, my land, for that son? No way. I might have been a pushover, but I was not that big of a wimp."

"Do you think maybe when Percy told PJ he wouldn't give him the property, PJ killed him?"

Her eyes widened. "That's entirely possible."

I could almost see the wheels turning in her head.

"Do you think I was poisoned too?"

"Why would you think that?"

"That night Percy died, I got really sick. That's why I didn't go after him when he tore out of the house."

"Do you think something was in the food?" I asked.

"It couldn't have been," she said. "Ty and Sally were with us, and neither of them got sick. Plus, I cooked everything from start to finish."

I pulled my hand away and turned the steering wheel into Helen's driveway.

"Was there anything else that might have been the culprit? Maybe some wine Percy might have gotten?"

Helen sat up straight in her seat as we came to a stop. "There wasn't wine, but there was a brand-new bottle of whiskey Percy brought home. He said he got it at the liquor store in town. But what if he got it from PJ?"

"Was PJ in town then?" I asked.

She shrugged. "I have no idea."

"Do you have any more of the whiskey?" I asked. "Maybe you could have the police test it for poison and fingerprints."

"I can check," she said. "I'm not entirely sure what Percy did with it."

I turned Mona off.

"Don't tell anyone I was drinking, okay?" she asked. "It's just, I'm a good Christian woman. It wouldn't look good for me to be known as a drunk."

I wanted to tell her she probably shouldn't get drunk in front of her friends if she didn't want them to know she got drunk. But it wasn't my place to judge.

"I won't say anything," I said. "But you might need to tell Jake since you got sick too."

She nodded. "When the time comes, I'll tell him."

15

Helen walked into the house before me and headed straight down the hallway to where I assumed was their bedroom. Maybe that's where Percy kept their alcohol. If they were trying to keep their friends from knowing they were drinkers, they likely wouldn't want it out in the kitchen where someone could stumble upon it.

Katie and Earl walked in right after me.

"How is she?" Katie asked.

"Surprisingly okay," I said. "She and I think PJ might have killed Percy."

Earl nodded. "We were talking about that too."

"But why wouldn't he have killed both of them?" Katie asked.

"I think he tried," I said, then regretted it immediately. I wasn't supposed to talk about their drinking. "I mean, maybe he would have come back for Helen, but something happened."

"Helen got sick that night, didn't she?" Katie asked.

"I think so." I shrugged. "Maybe?"

"She'd been drinking, hadn't she? She and Percy both."

Maybe Katie should be investigating. She seemed to catch on right away.

"Don't worry. I won't tell her we know." Katie laughed. "Everyone knows, but they all pretend not to. Iowa nice and all."

"Here comes trouble," Earl said, motioning toward the back door where Hank, PJ, and Ty all came in. "Maybe I should offer my services," he said to Katie. "If PJ didn't kill Percy, Helen will need my help."

"That's up to you," Katie said, squeezing his arm.

Earl nodded once and made his way over to Hank.

"What services?" I asked.

"Earl is an attorney," Katie said. "It's not something he wants to do anymore. But he keeps his license up to date for things like this."

"Hopefully, he can help Helen keep the farm." I added nothing about her failure to sign the prenup. That was her story to tell, not mine.

Earl, Hank, PJ, Ty, and Helen—who had come out from the bedroom looking defeated—gathered around a table in a sitting room off the back of the house for over an hour while people came and ate and went. I made sure I got some food, and when no one was looking, I stuffed a couple of rolls in my satchel for Penelope. She couldn't live on pig food alone.

When I was in the bathroom, checking my hair—which was still behaving itself—I remembered the towel smelled like vomit. This must have been where Helen had gotten sick. I picked up the towel and brought it to my nose, but this time it was fresh. She must have changed them out.

I peeked under the cabinets, but the only thing there was a little green cube, which I assumed was probably the mouse poison.

If they had whiskey, she could have easily slipped a bit of that little green cube into it. The cube did look like a couple of chunks were missing. That could have been from a mouse, though.

When I re-emerged, Jake was waiting his turn in the hall.

"Hello, Ellie," he said.

I smiled. "How are you?"

"Honestly, not great," he said. "It's not easy finding a murderer."

Tell me about it.

"I hear someone poisoned Percy," I said.

Jake frowned. "He had poison in his bloodstream, but his official cause of death was from a stab wound."

"Stab wound?" That blew my poisoning theory out the window.

"You probably didn't notice because he was on his stomach," he said. "But Percy had been stabbed in the stomach and bled out."

I remembered seeing the brown stain in the dirt the night I'd almost run right through the crime scene.

"So he was poisoned but didn't die from it?" I asked. "Do you know what kind of poison?"

Jake paused. "It's only natural to want to figure out who did this, especially because you've been accused. But we have the investigation under control, okay?"

"I know," I said. "I just feel bad because he died on my property, possibly even while I was there."

"You arrived around eight-thirty, right?"

"You have a good memory," I said. "Yeah, it was probably around then."

"The coroner said Percy died earlier in the evening. Before you were ever in town."

"Can you maybe spread that rumor for me?" I laughed but wasn't entirely joking.

"The town will learn to love you, just like they learned to love Esme."

"Why didn't they love her to begin with?" I shifted my weight from one foot to another. "Someone told me the Vanderwick women are trouble."

"Well, that might be true." He smiled. "Esme's family moved here when she was young, and from an early age, people thought Esme was a witch."

I laughed. "A witch? Why?" It took everything in me to keep my hand from reaching up to my hair.

People had called me a witch before. Not because I could do any actual magic, but because they'd never seen anyone with color-changing hair. In my mind, color-changing hair did not make someone a witch.

"When she was little, things that were broken would be fixed in ways a little girl couldn't possibly do on her own. She built your house with her own two hands. The garage and barn too. And in record time." Jake stopped and sighed. "Plus, she just seemed to make people feel better when she was around. It was like she could sense things and then fix them."

"But if she was a witch, it sounds like she was a good witch. Why wouldn't people like that?"

"It's not that they didn't like it. It was that they didn't understand it." Jake smiled. "But eventually, they came to depend on it. That's one reason everyone misses her so much. Besides the fact that she was one of the nicest people I've ever met."

"I wish I could have known her." I cleared my throat to keep the emotion out of my voice. "Why do you think she waited so long to send me anything?"

Jake's expression was sad. "Didn't Ty tell you? He was supposed to tell you all this."

I shook my head.

"She only just found out about you. No one in Cliff Haven knew you existed until earlier this year."

"How did she find out?"

"I don't know." Jake shook his head. "But the moment she did, she was on a quest to find you. Apparently, you moved around a lot."

"Since I can remember, I haven't been in one place for more than a few months."

"I'm so sorry." Jake looked down at his feet. "I wish we would have known sooner."

"Me too," I said. "But at least I'm here now."

He looked up. "At least you're here now." He smiled. "You know when I was asking you about the case and asked if you had any feelings about it."

I nodded.

"The reason I asked was because Esme often had feelings—intuition—about things." He shoved his hands down into his pockets and rocked back on his heels. "She helped with a lot of cases."

"The letter she sent said there wasn't much crime in Cliff Haven."

"Not much crime?" Jake let out a burst of laughter. "I guess she would have said that to get you to come. But Cliff Haven is just like any other town. There's crime. We just don't talk about it much, especially when we could solve the cases so handily."

"With Esme's feelings?"

Jake nodded.

"I wish I had feelings about things," I said.

"Don't worry," he said. "You don't have to be exactly like her."

"There you are," Deb said, coming down the hall.

"What's up?" Jake asked.

Deb held up a knife in her gloved hand. "I found the murder weapon."

Jake's eyes grew at the sight of the dried-up blood. So that's why he was inspecting my knives.

"I hoped it wouldn't be true," Jake said.

"Where did you find it?" I asked.

Deb sighed. "In the kitchen, with the other knives."

"And you think Helen did it?" I asked.

"You don't?" Jake asked.

"Why would Helen put the murder weapon back without cleaning it?" It seemed like a reasonable question. Especially since she'd laundered the towel. If she was trying to get away with murder, I would guess she would have cleaned the knife and left the towel dirty.

"People make mistakes all the time in crimes of passion," Deb said.

"But what about PJ—Percy's son?" I was grasping at straws.

"He's on our list of people to talk to," Jake said.

"Good, because he might have done it to get the farm."

"But why would he only kill Percy and not Helen too?" Deb asked, obviously not believing me.

"Maybe he tried," I said. "Helen was sick that night too. Maybe PJ poisoned them."

Deb laughed. "How would he have poisoned them? From the looks of things, it doesn't seem like Helen would invite him to dinner."

"It could have been in a drink he gave Percy." I sounded like a child trying to get out of trouble. But I couldn't let them arrest Helen for something she didn't do.

But did I know she didn't do it?

"That sounds pretty far-fetched and doesn't explain the knife," Deb said, still holding the sharp object up for us to see. "As far as we know, PJ has never been in Helen's house. If he killed Percy, how would he have gotten the knife back here? Plus, how do we know Helen got sick? She could be lying."

"It was on the towel," I said. "I smelled vomit on the towel in the bathroom the day I found Percy, and we were all over here."

"Can you show us the towel?" Deb asked.

"Well, it's not dirty anymore," I said, motioning toward the bathroom. "But maybe a forensic specialist can extract some of it. I know when I vomited once as a kid, my favorite hoodie never smelled the same."

"Even if he tried to poison them," Jake said, his voice kind. "That's not how Percy died."

"And Earl told me that Percy hadn't told Helen about PJ," Deb said. "That's why they were arguing at Fran's. Helen had to have come across that information herself."

My heart sank. So many signs pointed to Helen. More than what pointed to PJ.

I followed Jake and Deb back into the kitchen.

"I'm so sorry, Helen, but you're under arrest for the murder of your husband," Jake said.

Helen gaped at him. "I think I heard you wrong," she said. "Did you say I'm under arrest?"

"Please place your hands behind your back," Deb said.

Helen took a step back. "I did nothing wrong. I would never have hurt Percy, even if he deserved it."

"Don't make this harder than it has to be," Deb said.

Helen glanced at the door before she took off running.

Jake and Deb ran after her, but she was too fast.

"Wow," Ty said. "I haven't seen Aunt Helen run like that before."

"Not since high school," Katie said. "She still holds multiple school records. But her hips were too bad for her to continue in college."

PJ cleared his throat. "That's all fine and dandy. Now, if you would all kindly get off my property." He ignored me completely.

Ty looked like he might attack PJ again, but Earl grabbed his arm. "We'll get this figured out. Is there anything of value that needs to be secured before we leave?"

Ty shook his head. "I don't think so."

PJ followed us out, but instead of leaving, I turned and pointed a finger right into his nose.

"We need to talk," I said.

16

P J stepped out of the way and let me back in the house. "Please don't hurt me," he said. "This is none of your business."

"What are you playing at here?" I asked. "You and I both know your business makes plenty of money. You don't need this property."

PJ kept glancing up at my hair as if it might jump off my head and attack him.

"This farm is rightfully mine," he said. "My father has told me so my entire life."

"And yet, the will is only dated earlier this year," I said. I'd seen the date when I'd driven Helen home.

"It was just an updated will," PJ said. "I've always been the recipient of the farm should he die."

"But he changed his mind, didn't he?" I took a step toward him, hoping my intimidating act was working.

He took a step back. "No."

"And you didn't like that, so you thought you'd kill him before he could change the will back."

"That's not what happened."

"How did you get the knife back in the house?" I asked. "Did you come here during the funeral?"

"I was at the funer—oh my, it's happening again." He pointed at my head.

It felt almost freeing not to try to control my hair. I could see the red hue from the corner of my eye as it fell over my shoulders in waves.

"Tell me what happened," I said, trying to use his fear against him. But before he could answer, a knock at the door followed by Ty's voice interrupted.

PJ lunged toward the door, but I stepped in front of him.

"You will tell absolutely no one about my hair, do you understand?"

PJ nodded, his eyes wide. "Just don't hurt me."

I didn't respond before letting myself out the back door.

When I got back home, something was amiss. "Penelope?" I called when she didn't come out to greet me.

None of the doors were open or unlocked, the windows were all closed and latched, but I had the feeling that someone was inside. Had Helen run to my house?

My scalp tingled, but not enough to make me panic.

After the day I'd had, I didn't need any more drama. I needed a tall glass of ice water and a good yoga session. I pulled the small can of pepper spray out of my satchel, ready for someone to jump out at me.

"Penelope?" I climbed the stairs two at a time. Penelope wasn't in Dewdrop or Luna or Rainbow. Not in Firefly or Borealis either. When I finally got to Esme's room and opened the door, Penelope charged out.

I gathered her up in my arms, thankful she was okay. "How did you get in there?" I asked. She squealed until I put her down. She ran to the stairs and spun in a little circle.

I scooped her up again and took her downstairs.

She charged out the piggy door to relieve herself. When I reached the back door to make sure she was okay, she was running back toward me. She jumped back through the piggy door and ran right past me back to the stairs.

"Penelope," I said. "Are you okay?"

I chased her back to Esme's room where she sat in the doorway waiting for me.

It didn't take her warning oink for me to know my hair was changing. Something was off. But what?

I hurried to the bookcase and pushed the books aside to find my papers where I'd left them. I sighed in relief.

Everything looked to be in place, other than a few piles of poop.

"It's okay," I said. "You didn't mean to."

Penelope gave me her sad eyes. I bent down and cuddled her.

"It's really okay." I tried to comfort her. "Why don't I get it all cleaned up, and then we can forget all about it?"

Penelope grumbled.

I set to work cleaning the poop. It was already pretty

caked into the carpet, but with a bit of scrubbing and a lot of carpet cleaning solution, it came up.

"I brought you some rolls," I said, handing one to Penelope. She refused it and walked to a corner of the room. "I'm not mad at you. You didn't mean to poop in the house."

She didn't budge.

"Come on, let's go downstairs."

But she just kept her nose in the corner.

I walked over to find what looked like a small hole in the wall. "What's this?"

Penelope moved out of the way. The carpet was pushed down in a little bed where it seemed like Penelope had been standing guard. Or rather, laying, guard.

The wall around the hole seemed normal. The hole looked like one that a doorstop would make if the door had been slammed open too hard. But there was no door adjacent to the hole.

"What should I look for," I wondered aloud.

Penelope sniffed the wall and oinked.

I reluctantly put my finger in the hole to find a small nodule that compressed like a button when I pushed.

A rush of cool air hissed from the gap created by the nearest bookshelf and the wall.

"A secret passage?" I asked Penelope, who hurried to the gap and oinked excitedly.

I slid my fingers into the gap, and the bookshelf swung toward me easily. Small lights cast a golden glow up a beautifully finished wooden staircase that curved toward the attic.

Every step brought increased anticipation. I could feel

my hair changing from the scalp. I pulled a strand toward my face to find hues of pink and gold had replaced the red.

At the top of the stairs was a small yet open space. Windows allowed views of all sides of the house. An over-sized leather chair with a soft knit blanket and a small wooden table sat in the center of the room, the chair facing the far window.

A notebook sat on the table, a pen acting as a page marker. I knew without looking—this was Esme's private journal. Something she may or may not have wanted me to see.

Did she think I'd ever be here? Sitting in her chair? Or were her intentions to let it go dormant? Did Ty know about this place?

I sat in the chair, curling my legs up underneath me and pulling Penelope onto my lap. Whatever sense of danger I'd gotten when I was downstairs had completely evaporated. This room was pure joy, comfort, and warmth.

Outside, the sun was setting over the horizon—lights from the occasional vehicle poked through the growing darkness. I must have fallen asleep because the next thing I knew, it was morning, and Penelope was nudging me awake.

"What time is it?" I asked, knowing perfectly well I was about to be late for my shift at the café.

I draped the blanket over the back of the chair and gave the room one last glance before rushing downstairs and securing the bookshelf back into place.

My hair had stayed the golden-pink, so I tied it back into a bun and covered it with a scarf. A new pair of yoga pants, a fresh tank top, a kiss on Penelope's head, and I was off.

"Cutting it close," Bex said when I walked through the door, the bells jingling giving me away.

The clock said I had a minute to spare. "Sorry, I overslept."

"Can you get the farmer's table," she said, motioning to where five men sat waiting for their coffee.

I poured their coffee without spilling on anyone and got their orders into the kitchen in record time. The men were quiet this morning, all seemingly lost in thought. Ty sat between Hank and Earl while William and George completed the circle.

"Anything good in the paper today?" William asked Earl.

"Nothing new," Earl said.

"Surprised they didn't put something in about Helen," George said.

Hank and Ty both turned his way.

"Not that I want them to," George added quickly.

"Helen didn't kill Percy," Hank said. "I'm betting it was PJ."

"But they found the knife in Aunt Helen's house," Ty said.

"She never locks her house," Hank said. "Anyone could have put it there."

"And if she did it, why would she have put the knife back without cleaning it first?" Earl asked. "None of it makes any sense."

"That's why I think PJ did it," Hank said, nodding.

Ty shifted in his seat. "I went to see PJ last night at Aunt Helen's."

Hank looked at him. "Why on God's green earth would you do such a thing?"

"I just wanted to talk to him. See if he'd tell me anything."

"And did he?"

The rest of the men acted as if they weren't listening, but just like I was, they were riveted.

Ty hadn't given away that he knew anything about my hair, so I was pretty sure PJ hadn't told him.

"He said he's going to develop the property," Ty said. "He has his own development company out of Des Moines."

"I thought he was from Chicago," Hank said.

"And Ellie thought he was from Colorado," Ty whispered as they both looked my way. I focused on rolling silverware into napkins and acting as if I couldn't hear a thing. "But when I looked him up, he's been in Des Moines for years."

I wanted to interject. No, he hadn't been in Des Moines for years. Maybe a year. But before that, he was in Colorado for at least three months. With me. We even lived together the better part of two of those months. At one point, I thought he might be the one for me. That's why my hair turned green when I caught him cheating on me. I was more jealous than I was mad.

"If he's out of Des Moines, you probably know him then," Hank said, his voice edgier than usual.

"I may have spoken to someone at his company," Ty

said. "But I had no idea the owner was practically my cousin."

"There's no practically about it," Hank said into his coffee, obviously tired of the conversation. "You're cousins even if you're not blood-related."

Ty retreated into silence. I rolled a dozen more silverware packs before anyone else came in. When the door opened, letting in the cool autumn air, not even the fun jingle bells could make me smile.

PJ stood there, and he had his eyes set on me.

He approached carefully and stood as far away from me as he could manage while still being close enough to have a semi-private conversation. It was my turn to have people listen in on my conversation. The men at the farmer table were not in the least subtle about their eavesdropping.

"I think we got off on the wrong foot," PJ said, sucking in a breath. "I'd like to take you out to dinner tonight if you'd be up for it."

I didn't even want to see the looks on the farmers' faces. I had enough to contemplate at the thought that this man—the one who had seen my biggest weakness —wanted to take me out on a date. I'd never had someone come back after an incident. Not a foster family. Not a friend. Not an employer. Not a boyfriend. Not once.

My heart skipped at the thought. Then I remembered the reason my hair had changed in the first place.

"I take it you and the brunette didn't work out." I had to be careful with my words, or they could spur my emotions and my hair.

"That was a total mistake," PJ said. "She kissed me. You walked in at the exact wrong time."

"It looked pretty mutual," I said but started to doubt my memory. I hadn't given him a chance to explain himself before my hair had gone all wonky.

"Trust me. It wasn't." PJ smiled and shoved his hands deeper into the pockets of his fancy-pants jeans. "And if it wasn't for—uh—" He glanced back at the farmers. "—well, you know. The argument afterward."

I nodded. The argument was me completely freaking out. Well, my hair, at least.

"If it wasn't for that, I thought we would have been together a long time. I'd even picked out a ring."

My heart dropped. He'd picked out a ring? I could feel my hair pulling itself into ringlets under my scarf.

"I thought we would have been together a long time too," I finally said.

"So you'll go to dinner with me tonight?"

I stood, and he took a tentative step toward me. "Yes, I'll go out with you."

He held his arms open, and I practically fell into them. I'd forgotten how amazing his hugs were.

"I'll pick you up around seven," he said, pulling away with a flickering gaze to my hair.

"Seven it is," I said. "Do I need to dress up?"

"I figured we'd go a couple of towns over. So maybe something nicer than yoga pants." He looked down at the pants I wore.

I nodded. I only had one pair of jeans, but they'd have to do.

When PJ had gone, Earl came up next to me.

"If you need something to wear, I'm sure Katie would be delighted to help," he whispered. "Just be careful, that one might be a murderer."

First, PJ asked me out. Now Earl was acting like I was his daughter. This was shaping up to be the best day.

Katie was on my front porch with two suitcases when I got home. "Earl told me you had a date and might need some help."

"Thanks," I said. I held out a hand with my measly tips. "After food and bills, I definitely don't have money for clothes. But the good news is the town is coming around. I only got nine pennies today."

"This is all you got in tips today?" Katie asked.

I shrugged and opened the door. "It was a slow day."

"And what do you mean you only got nine pennies?"

"The day after Sally accused me of killing Percy, I got twenty-eight. It's slowly decreasing."

Katie looked furious. "If this town doesn't appreciate my wait staff, maybe I'll just have to shut the café down for a few days."

"It's okay." I felt bad for saying anything. I should have learned by now when to keep my mouth shut. "I just wanted you to know why I don't have any nice clothes yet."

"A woman is not defined by her clothes." Katie opened a suitcase. "But a good outfit can make a woman's day brighter."

The clothes she pulled out were beautiful. They probably cost more than my entire paycheck last year.

"Why don't you try this first," Katie held up a black pleated shift dress.

I hurried into the small downstairs bathroom—one I'd never used—and slipped the dress on. My hair reacted by tightening into a low chignon but stayed white.

When I emerged, Katie clapped her hands together. "I don't even know why I brought the rest. I knew this one would be perfect. And your hair looks amazing."

I blushed.

"Now, let's talk about shoes."

By the time Katie was done with me, I looked like an upgraded version of myself. She let me borrow some statement jewelry that had sparkly little stars all over, a pair of black heels I could barely walk in, and did my makeup in a way I would never have had the guts to try.

I tried my hardest not to mess anything up before PJ arrived.

When there was a knock at the door, I was surprised to find Ty.

His face was in utter shock. "You look gorgeous."

"Thank you." I tried not to blush. "What are you doing here? PJ is picking me up soon."

"That's why I'm here," Ty said. "You need to be careful with PJ."

"I've known PJ a long time. Why would I need to be careful?"

Ty looked behind him as if PJ might somehow sneak up on him. "I think PJ might have killed Percy."

A burst of heat radiated toward my scalp. I closed my eyes and took a deep breath. My hair could not change. Even if it was as paranoid as Ty.

"What makes you think that?" I asked when I felt like I'd regained control of my hair.

"I know Aunt Helen," he said. "She would never have killed Uncle Percy. She may have been angry with him, but she loved him more than anything. PJ is only looking for money. I talked to him about it. He wants to put in luxury homes. Lots of them. He asked me to join him."

"How would you join him?" I asked.

"With my father's farm." Ty looked down at his boots. "It's practically my farm at this point. I'd just need dad to sign off."

"If you think he killed Percy, why would you go into business with him?"

"Going into business is better than going on a date," Ty said.

"I'll be okay," I said. "There's no reason he'd want to hurt me."

Ty reached out and rubbed my bare arm. "I just don't want to see anything happen to you."

Goosebumps made their way up my neck. He was so handsome. More handsome than PJ. The thought of him in a towel flashed through my mind.

"You know, I thought maybe you and I could go on a date sometime," Ty said. "But I guess I missed my chance."

"You're with Sally," I said.

He shrugged. "Sometimes."

Lights from a truck came pulling up the driveway.

"I guess I should go so you can get on with your date."

Part of me didn't want him to go. But PJ knew me. He knew about my hair and still wanted to take me on a date.

"Have a good night," I said as Ty walked to his truck.

"You too," he said. "And be careful."

PJ threw up a wave to Ty as Ty pulled out of the driveway. It was only at that point I realized PJ was driving the truck I'd seen in town my first day at the diner. The one that said Des Moines Developers on the side.

If he was already in town . . .

"Wow, Ellie," he said. "You are stunning. Iowa looks good on you."

"Uh, thanks," I said, still lost in thought over the case.

"Should we head out?" he said.

I hesitated. Maybe going with him was a bad idea.

"I just need to get my purse," I said. "I'll be right back."

I turned back into the house and ran upstairs. I'd almost forgotten my phone, and if something happened, I'd definitely need it.

I carefully unzipped the little black clutch Katie had let me borrow and stuck the phone inside along with my pepper spray.

"Okay, I'm ready," I said, opening the door. "See you

later, Penelope," I called behind me, but she was probably off in dreamland.

"You still have Penelope?" PJ said. "I've missed that little piggy."

He opened the truck door for me, and I waited to feel anything—any sense of danger. But my hair was surprisingly neutral.

Maybe I had nothing to worry about after all.

"I've missed you too, you know," he said when he got into the driver's seat.

"Really?" I asked, just then noticing the hideous shirt he wore. The brown and green paisley print did nothing for his dark complexion.

"When everything happened—" He glanced up at my hair. "—I freaked out. I've just never seen anything like that before."

"Oh, you've never seen someone's hair change color because of their emotions?" I laughed.

He laughed too. "Nope. But when I think about it more, I kind of like it."

"You do?"

"Sure, I mean, it's definitely unique." He paused. "Is it magical or something?"

I shrugged. "No. But that would be cool, right?"

"I guess it would depend on what the magic did." He laughed nervously. "I haven't believed in magic since I was six and believed in Santa Claus."

"Wait," I said, turning in my seat toward him. "You don't believe in Santa Claus?"

He smiled and reached a hand out for mine. "You're adorable."

Ty may have been smoking hot, but PJ was gentle and kind. There was no way he killed Percy.

"How is your mom doing with Percy's death?"

"She's beside herself," he said. "I don't think it helps that she didn't feel like she could come to his funeral. They weren't married, but they were soul mates."

"Why didn't he just leave Helen?" I asked. It only seemed logical.

PJ shrugged. "I always wondered that myself. He was with us more than he was with her. He told her he had farming shows to go to. It's surprising she never caught on." He turned onto a highway. "Or maybe she did. And maybe she killed him."

"How long have you been in town?" I asked.

"Only since yesterday, I barely made the funeral."

But I knew I'd seen this same truck my first day on the job. What was he trying to pull?

When there was a lull in the conversation, PJ turned on music that he and I used to listen to. Not my favorite, but it reminded me of our time together.

"I'm sorry about your dad," I said. "He didn't deserve to die."

He squeezed my hand. "Thanks."

We drove the rest of the way in silence, holding hands.

***

"How did you find this place?" I asked when PJ opened the truck door and helped me out. Grazie was a beautiful little Italian restaurant that could have easily been missed if you weren't looking for it.

"Technically, I own it," he said. "The property, anyway. The restaurant rents the space."

"I didn't realize when we dated that you had a business in Des Moines."

When we walked in, the smell of Italian herbs and fresh bread hit my nose and made my mouth water. I didn't realize how much I missed real food. Well, other than breakfast food.

"I have three companies," he said. "One here, one in Denver, and one in Chicago. I rarely tell people because they think I'm rich."

"Aren't you?" I asked with a nervous laugh.

He smiled. "I guess I am."

The hostess seated us in a half-circle booth overlooking a beautiful stream with an outdoor seating area surrounded by white twinkle lights.

We ordered our dinner and wine and munched on the bread and oil the waitress brought as an appetizer.

PJ took my hand as we watched the stream bubble outside.

"So you're going to create luxury housing?" I asked, trying to keep any indication of my thoughts out of my voice.

"Modern luxury housing. Something Iowa desperately needs." He looked over at me. "You know, that's part of the reason I wanted to take you to dinner tonight."

He rubbed a thumb over the top of my hand.

"I wanted to know if you would like to go into business with me."

My chest compressed as if all the air in my lungs had disappeared.

"That's why you brought me here?"

"Well, that and because I missed you." He looked sincere. "But if you would go in with me, our two farms would make quite a lot of money. And if Ty could convince his father—"

"Hank will never agree to it," I interrupted.

"Ty knows farming is a dying industry." PJ ignored me. "He wants out of this town just as much as you do."

"I don't want out of the town," I said. "I like it there."

"You do?" PJ let go of my hand and took a sip of his wine. "That's surprising."

"Why do you say that?"

"You just don't strike me as the settling down type. Never have."

"Then why would you have been looking for rings?" I asked. If there was one thing I hated, it was being lied to.

"I thought I could get you to settle down." He shrugged. "Oh hey, speaking of Ty." PJ stood and greeted his cousin, who was sitting down at a booth across from us.

Wearing an almost identical paisley shirt except his was brown and blue.

With Sally.

18

"Looking good," PJ said with a wink.

"This old rag?" Ty joked back before flashing me a quick smile.

"Why don't you join us?" PJ said. "We were just getting started."

The look on Sally's face echoed my feelings. Neither of us wanted to sit together.

"That sounds like fun," Ty said without consulting his date.

PJ motioned for me to move closer to him while Ty pushed Sally into the booth toward me.

"Maybe we shouldn't intrude on their date," Sally said. "It looks like they were having a private conversation."

"Just talking about developing the land," PJ said.

Ty's eyes widened. "With her?"

"Her land is right next to mine," PJ said. "It would only make sense she be included in the development plans." He sipped his wine. "Of course, it would have made things much simpler had she not shown up, and the land would have reverted to you."

I frowned, and that twinge of guilt returned.

"Esme wanted Ellie to have it, not me," Ty said, hurt threaded through every word.

"Esme loved you," Sally said, trying to comfort him, but he shrugged her off.

"It doesn't matter," Ty said. "I think I'm close to convincing my dad to give me the land."

I nearly got whiplash looking over at him. I couldn't picture Hank handing over a piece of property he seemed so proud of.

"Perfect," PJ said. "And when he agrees, I'll pay you handsomely for it."

"But I'm not going to sell you my land," I said. My hair follicles felt like little knives stabbing into my head. My hair wanted to change, but I couldn't let it. Not with Ty and Sally around. "The land belonged to my grandmother, and I plan on staying there as long as I can."

"That's entirely up to you," PJ said, his voice unaffected. "But your property value will tank when there are houses all around."

"I don't care about my property value," I said. "And farming is not a dying industry. It keeps our country running. Now, if you'll please let me out of this booth, I need to use the restroom."

PJ slid out but grabbed my hand on my way by and kissed my cheek gently. "I wasn't trying to upset you," he said. "I wanted to show you the opportunity. I was doing you a favor."

I wanted to tell him where to put his favor, but instead, I took a deep breath and smiled. "I appreciate you looking out for my best interests."

Ty looked like he might vomit, but Sally squeezed his hand, drawing his attention away from me.

"I think I'll go to the bathroom too," Sally said, shimmying her way out of the booth carefully so as not to show the entire restaurant her lady parts. Her skirt was tighter than a brand-new exercise band in a cold room and barely covered her butt.

I didn't wait for her to follow. I needed to be alone, and she was not helping the matter. Though, when had Sally ever helped the matter?

I locked myself into the first stall—the cleanest one, scientifically—before she even made her way through the doors.

In fact, she still hadn't come in when I re-emerged.

I peeked out the door, but she wasn't there.

I sighed and went to the sink.

My hair was frizzy at the temples, but all in all, it was keeping its shape in the chignon. The color was on the verge of transition from white to blonde but quickly reverted back when I splashed water on my face.

When I glanced in the mirror one more time, I nearly screamed in horror. All the beautiful makeup Katie had expertly painted onto my face was dripping and smudged. I'd totally forgotten. I brought nothing with me for touch-ups, so my only option was to remove it altogether.

By the time I looked like my usual plain self, my stomach was grumbling.

PJ and Ty had already started eating while mine and Sally's food sat in our places. Sally still wasn't back.

"What happened to you?" PJ said.

I acted as if I had no idea what he was talking about. "Just had to use the ladies' room."

"Where's Sally?" Ty asked.

"I'm not sure." I slid in and took a big bite of my spaghetti. The noodles were homemade and fresh. I'd never been to Italy, but I imagined it would taste like this.

Sally returned to the table about fifteen minutes later, looking like she'd run a marathon.

"Everything okay?" Ty asked, standing and letting her slide in next to me.

"Why wouldn't it be?" Sally snapped back.

Ty shrugged her off and continued his conversation with PJ about all the things they could do with the land.

"Why don't you want to sell Esme's farm?" Sally whispered beside me. "No one wants you here."

I steadied myself before I responded. "I know not everyone wants me here, but I'd like to think there are some people who do."

"Katie and Earl don't matter," she said. "Just because they've taken you in to fill some hole their daughter left in their hearts doesn't mean they won't drop you the minute she comes back to town."

Her words stung. "Hank and Nancy and Amy and Fran and Helen like me too."

Sally acted like she didn't hear me as she finished the rest of what was in her wine glass and refilled it almost to the top.

"It's too bad PJ's engaged," she said. "He's quite the catch."

Engaged? I swallowed.

"Oh, he didn't tell you?" She laughed. "These men will do anything to get us to go along with their plans."

"What plans does Ty have you going along with?" I asked, turning the tables on her.

She nearly choked on the bite of food she'd just taken.

"You okay?" Ty asked when her coughing became incessant.

She pushed him to get out of the booth and made a beeline for the bathroom.

Ty sat back down as if nothing had happened.

"So I hear you're engaged," I said to PJ.

"I don't know what that has to do with anything," PJ said. "But, yes, I'm engaged."

"Then what was this?" I asked, fighting the tears that were forming in my eyes. "Why did you ask me on a date?"

"A date?" He shook his head. "This wasn't a date. This was a business meeting."

"Do you hold the hands of all the people you take on business meetings?" I asked.

"Or kiss their cheeks?" Ty murmured.

"Okay, now," PJ held up his hands. "I think you're blowing this out of proportion." He glanced up at my hair, but his gaze returned to my face.

"Can you please let me out?" I asked Ty. He slid out and held out a hand to help me out of the booth. "I'll get my own ride home." I threw my last thirty dollars on the table. "Have a nice life and stay away from my farm."

The fresh air filled my lungs and helped keep the tears in my eyes from falling down my face. I was so stupid to think PJ had wanted to rekindle something.

And I'd made a complete fool of myself in front of Ty.

I pulled out my phone and looked up ride-sharing apps. Surely, I'd be able to get some sort of car, right?

Except I had no money. I didn't believe in credit cards, and even if I had a bank account, there wouldn't be any money in it to pay with a debit card.

How was I so stupid to believe PJ? Why had I trusted him?

I glanced around. I was in the middle of nowhere. I had no one's phone number and no ride.

Except . . . my fingers fumbled through my clutch. It should be there.

When my fingers came in contact with the paper, I let out a sigh of relief.

Jake's name and cell phone number were on the card he'd given me the first time we met.

I typed the number into my phone but hesitated to push the send button. Was it weird that I was calling him? What if he was busy? I didn't even know if he was dating anyone. Or married. He wasn't wearing a ring—not even one like all the farmers wore—but maybe that didn't matter.

I swallowed and hit send. I had no other choice.

"This is Jake," he said, his voice tired.

"Uh, hi," I said. "It's Ellie."

"Is everything okay?" Jake's voice perked up.

"Everything's fine." I looked around. "Well, kind of. I went on a date with PJ—or at least I thought it was a date, but he is apparently in a relationship. Anyway, I walked out but then realized I didn't have a way to get home."

"You need a ride?" I could hear him rustling around with something in the background. "I'll be right there. Where are you?"

"Ellie?" Ty said from behind me.

"Who's that?" Jake asked.

"It's Ty," I said.

"Ty went on your date with you?" Jake asked.

"No, Ty and Sally just happened to show up at the same place."

Sally was rushing out of the restaurant calling after Ty.

"Who are you talking to?" Ty asked.

"Jake," I said. "He's going to pick me up."

"I can take you home," Ty said.

"I'm sorry to bother you, Jake," I said into the phone. "Ty said he'd take me home."

Jake didn't respond immediately.

"Are you there?" I asked.

"I'm here," Jake said. "Are you sure you want to go home with Ty?"

"Sally's here too," I said. "It'll be okay."

"This may sound weird, but can you call and let me know you made it home safely?"

I didn't want to think about it too hard, but that was a rather fatherly thing to say.

"Yeah, I'll call when I get there."

"Great," Jake said. "Thanks."

I hung up, and Ty led Sally and me over to a car that looked more Aspen than Iowa.

"When did you get this?" I asked. "Where did your truck go?"

"He bought it today," Sally said, hanging off his shoulder. "I think it suits him much more than that beat-up old truck."

I didn't mention that I'd seen him in his truck only a couple of hours ago.

Ty held the door open and pulled the seat forward so I could slip into the teeny tiny back seat. I'd never been in such a fancy car.

Ty and Sally sat in silence as we made our way back to Cliff Haven. The silence was fine with me. My mind was still trying to come to terms with what happened.

When we got back to the house, Ty let me out of the car, then looked in at Sally and said, "I'll be right back."

Sally didn't respond.

"You don't have to walk me to my door," I said. "I'm perfectly capable."

"It's okay," Ty said. "I want to."

I fumbled to get the keys out of my purse as Ty stood by and waited. I was almost certain Sally was watching our every move.

"For what it's worth, you didn't deserve to be treated like that tonight," Ty said. "If I'd known PJ was going to do that, I would have tried to talk him out of it."

I pivoted and looked Ty right in the eye. "Since when are the two of you so chummy?" My tone was far less kind than his had been. "I thought you hated him."

"We have some common interests, that's all."

"Yeah, like destroying the farms that mean the world to your family just to make a profit."

I almost didn't care if my hair was changing. But in the dim porch light, Ty probably wouldn't have noticed, anyway.

"I know it might be hard to understand." Ty's voice was still kind. "You've been able to travel. To go where you want, do as you please. Me? I've been stuck here my entire life. I haven't even been out of state. This is my chance to do something I want to do."

"Like what?"

Ty shook his head. "That's just it—I don't even know. But the money PJ's promised will allow me to do almost anything." Ty looked back at the car. "It already has."

"He's already paid you?"

"No," Ty said, his eye twitching. "But he's promised to the minute I get my father to sign off."

"You know him better than I do, but I don't think Hank's going to give you the farm."

Ty huffed. "It doesn't matter, does it? You own a farm. You could sell it, but you want to stay here. It makes no sense to me."

"I guess just like you're tired of staying, I'm tired of going. Tired of running. I'm happy to be settled." I pushed the key into the lock. "Thank you for the ride."

"Any time," Ty said. "And by the way, you look more beautiful without the makeup."

He walked away, leaving me standing in the doorway, gaping at him.

I carefully hung Katie's dress and put the shoes back in the box she'd brought them in. It was nice to get gussied up every once in a while, but it was even nicer to be back in my yoga pants.

Penelope curled up in my lap when I made my way back up to the attic room. I'd retrieved the paperwork from behind the books. I needed to read it.

I made it about three pages before I fell asleep.

19

I woke to someone yelling my name. Actually, multiple people yelling my name.

I dropped the papers that hadn't already made their way to the floor, gathered up Penelope, hurried down the stairs, and out the secret door. No one was in Esme's bedroom, but voices were just outside in the hall.

I yanked the door open to find Katie in tears, her voice hoarse as she yelled my name one last time.

"Katie," I said. "I'm right here."

Katie gasped and wrapped me up in a big bear hug.

"I found her," Katie yelled down the stairs.

"What time is it?" I asked.

"It's almost two in the morning." She released me.

"And might I ask why you're in my house at two in the morning?"

Penelope leaned against my ankles, obviously still tired and utterly unfazed by the emotion surrounding her.

"We thought you were dead," Katie said.

Jake and Earl bounded up the stairs—Jake taking two at a time.

"You were supposed to call me," Jake said. "Why didn't you call me?"

Oops. "I'm so sorry. I'm not used to answering to anyone," I said.

Earl looked at me. "But you have to learn. You're part of this town now, and whether you like it or not, people care about you."

"You're here because I didn't call? Couldn't you have just called Ty and confirmed that he dropped me off? Why would you think I was dead?"

Jake and Earl exchanged a loaded look.

"Ty and PJ are in the hospital," Jake said. "Ty called to tell us he saw Helen. When he followed her, she broke into her house." Jake stopped and took a breath. "I told him to wait. It only took me seven minutes to get there. But by that time, Helen was dead, and Ty and PJ were unconscious."

"Helen's dead?" A wave of emotion washed over me. Before I could say anything else, I ducked into the nearest bathroom. My hair was changing faster than I could control. The tight black curls were back within seconds. I could only hope Jake, Katie, and Earl hadn't seen them.

Katie knocked on the door. "Hey, sweetie? You okay?"

I took a few deep breaths, but my hair was only getting worse.

"Ellie?" Earl's voice was calm. "If you're worried about your hair, you don't have to be."

My head turned faster than my neck preferred. Had I heard him right?

"Ellie," Katie's sweet voice was there again. "Esme had it too—the hair changing thing."

I slowly opened the door. None of them flinched at the sight of my hair. They didn't even look surprised.

"That's better," Katie said. "Now, are you okay?"

Helen was dead. Ty and PJ were unconscious. "Are PJ and Ty going to be okay?"

"They were both shot," Jake said. "As far as I know, they're in surgery."

"But what happened?" I asked, reaching up to touch my hair, trying not to feel self-conscious.

"It looked like PJ stabbed Helen—similar to the way Percy was stabbed—then shot Ty and then himself."

I pursed my lips to keep an I-told-you-so from coming out.

"I know. You told me. I wish I had looked into it more closely." Jake raked a hand through his hair. "From what we've gathered, PJ had plans to develop Percy and Helen's land. The minute Percy signed his new will, PJ went through with his plan to kill Helen and Percy. Only the poison didn't work. We think a bottle of whiskey was the culprit. He gave it to Percy as a thank you gift for the will."

"Helen got sick but didn't die," I said.

"Right," Jake said. "When Percy left the house, PJ followed him and stabbed him in your cornfield."

"Then he stabbed Helen tonight?" I asked. "How do you know it was him?" I didn't want to imply that it could have been Ty, but it was hard not to ask the question.

"Ty saw it happen," Jake said. "He was on the phone with dispatch, and you could hear Helen scream while Ty was whispering. There was a bunch of blood on PJ's shirt that indicated the spray pattern of the knife wound, and his hand was covered in blood."

"Was Ty trying to save her? Did he have the gun?"

"We're unclear where the gun came from at this point," Jake said. "Hank didn't think it was Ty or Helen's gun. It might have been PJ's."

I shook my head. "PJ hated guns." I couldn't believe I was standing up for him, but they couldn't go on without the truth.

"That's good to know," Jake said, jotting a note down in his pocket notebook. "I don't want to put any pressure on you, but do you happen to have any feeling about this?"

"Like what kind of feeling?"

Katie squeezed my hand. "Esme used to get feelings about things. She said it was almost like her hair knew things she couldn't possibly know."

"Her hair?" I asked. "I mean, sometimes mine warns me of danger, but I've never heard it *say* anything."

"Has it warned you of any danger since you've been here?" Katie asked.

I tried to think back, but I didn't remember it doing so. "No, I'm sorry. I was with Ty and PJ tonight, and my hair was practically on its best behavior."

"Were they acting strangely at all?" Jake asked.

"Other than being much friendlier than I'd expect," I said. "Not really."

"Friendlier how?"

"They were in cahoots to develop the two farms." I shook my head. "I thought PJ wanted to take me on a date

—I hung your clothes in the closet, by the way," I said to Katie. "But he only wanted to get me in on the plan."

"What did he offer you?" Earl asked.

"He didn't say exactly, only that I'd be very rich," I said. "I shut him down before he could get into specifics."

"That's my girl," Katie said. "Esme would be so proud."

Sally's words echoed in my head. Was Katie only being friendly because she missed her daughter?

"I find it hard to believe Ty had Hank's approval to develop the farm," Earl said.

"I think he was still working on convincing Hank," I said. "But I think PJ had already paid him some because Ty was driving a brand new sports car."

Jake nodded. "We found it at Sally's house."

"Speaking of," Katie said. "Has someone talked to Sally?"

"Deb has," Jake said. "Sally's at the hospital."

"We should get over there too," I said.

Penelope let out an excited oink.

"Sorry, sweetie." I got down on my knees and pulled her into my lap. "I'm going to have to leave you here. I'll be home soon." I kissed her snout, and she seemed satisfied with that answer.

"I'll drive," Jake said.

Within minutes we were loaded in Jake's personal pickup, Earl in the front, Katie and me in the back. The trip to the hospital took the better part of an hour. When we reached the city lights, I realized how much I'd missed them.

Being in the middle of nowhere had its advantages, but I missed the city's sights and sounds. People bustling about talking on phones or to the person next to them always made me feel like I was part of something, even if that wasn't the case.

The hospital was big and beautiful but still had that typical disinfectant smell.

Ty and PJ's rooms were right next door to one another. Both men were out of surgery. A woman held PJ's hand at his bedside. Her back was to us, but I figured she was probably his fiancée.

I wrapped my arms around my middle and tried to keep my wits about me. PJ and I had been over for a long time.

Though some of these people knew about my hair, the hospital staff didn't. I pulled the hood of my sweatshirt up to cover it just in case I couldn't control it.

"Hey Sally," Jake said when he led us into the room.

Sally stood and practically threw herself into Jake's arms, sobbing.

He didn't look even a tiny bit surprised. "How's he doing?"

"He's alive," she said between sobs. "For now."

Ty looked a lot better than PJ. PJ had tubes all over him, whereas Ty looked relatively normal.

"The doctors gave him some pretty powerful pain medication after the surgery," Hank said, walking in behind us. He held two drink carriers, each with four cups of coffee in them. "They said he got lucky."

Jake pulled away from Sally, but she was still hanging onto his arm. She looked almost unrecognizable without makeup or her hair teased up. She wore a plain pair of jeans and a high school volleyball t-shirt that had seen better days.

Earl took the coffees while Katie wrapped Hank in a big hug. "I'm so sorry about Helen."

Hank nodded, tears in his eyes. "I just can't believe she's gone. Why would she have gone back? It makes no sense."

Jake nodded, taking a coffee Earl was handing out.

I also took one, thankful for the caffeine. My hair energized from the first sip, almost like it was humming a quiet tune.

He was right. It didn't make sense. Unless Helen was going back to the house to kill PJ, and it backfired on her.

Immediately, I felt horrible for thinking ill of the dead.

"We'll figure it out," Jake said. "Just as soon as Ty wakes up."

"What if he doesn't remember," Sally said. "I've heard of people not remembering things like this."

"Then I'll just have to revert back to finding clues," Jake said. "But from the looks of things, there's not much to find."

"What do you mean?" Hank asked.

"The way we found them told the story pretty clearly," Jake said. "Helen was the victim of a stabbing, similar to Percy's. It looks like PJ was the culprit. Then Ty and PJ struggled over a gun, and they both ended up getting shot."

Jake left out the part about it looking like PJ tried to kill himself.

"Speaking of, how is PJ?" Jake asked.

Sally let out a loud sob startling me so much I almost spilled my coffee on myself.

"PJ won't make it," Hank said. "His mother hasn't arrived yet to make the final decision."

"Who's in there with him?" Jake asked.

Hank shrugged.

"It's probably his fiancée," I said.

"Wait, he had a fiancée and took you on a date?" Katie asked, her eyes widening.

"Remember, he was only taking me to dinner to discuss the development deal," I said.

"Right," Katie said, her tone angry.

"Development deal?" Hank asked. "What development deal?"

I didn't feel like it was my place to tell him about it if Ty hadn't already, but everyone was looking at me expectantly.

"He and Ty were talking about developing the two farms, and PJ wanted to know if I wanted in on it since I'm right next door," I said, confusion coming over Hank's face.

"Ty and PJ?" Hank asked.

"She's a liar," Sally said. "Ty hated PJ. Wanted nothing to do with him."

I waited for her to burst out laughing because she had to be joking.

But she didn't. Her glare stayed trained on my face.

"You were at dinner, right?" I said. "They acted like they were best friends."

"You're lying," Sally said. "PJ was threatening Ty. He said if Ty didn't do what he said, he'd kill him."

Everyone was looking at me. "That-that's not what happened."

I couldn't figure out why she was lying.

"And it looks like he followed through with his promise," Sally said. "Thank goodness Ty didn't die."

"Nope," Ty said, his voice hoarse. "Not dead."

Sally dropped Jake's arm and fell to her knees next to Ty's bed. She scooped up his hand and kissed it. "I'm so glad you're okay."

He pulled his hand from hers. "I'm fine."

She looked slightly jilted and got to her feet with a huff.

"Ty, can you clear all of this up?" Hank said.

Ty looked groggy but nodded. "What do you need to know?"

Jake pulled out a pen and pad of paper from his jeans pocket and sat in the chair Sally had just vacated. "Do you remember what happened last night?"

"It's kind of a blur," Ty said. "I know I went on a date with Sally. We saw PJ and Ellie there too. Then I took Ellie home in my new car."

"You have a new car?" Hank asked. "How'd you get a new car?"

"I bought it." Ty's gaze went to Hank, who had his arms crossed over his chest.

"I think what he's trying to ask is with what money?" Jake said.

"Since Esme died, you haven't been getting your monthly paychecks," Hank said. "And I haven't but paid you a fair living wage for your work at the farm. So how in the name of all things holy can you afford a brand-new car?"

"I was going to talk to you," Ty said. "If you knew how much they were offering, I knew you'd make the deal."

Everyone looked from Ty to Sally.

"But I thought you said you wouldn't sell the farm to PJ, right?" Sally said. She was a terrible actress, and it was obvious she was trying to get Ty on board with her lie. "You hated PJ, right?"

"Well, I didn't like him much," Ty said. "He wasn't nice to Ellie. But we were going to do business."

Sally looked like she might explode.

"Let's get back to last night," Jake said, breaking the

awkward tension in the room. "You took Ellie home, and then what happened?"

"He came home with me," Sally said.

Ty closed his eyes as if he was either in pain or frustrated.

"I went over to Sally's," Ty confirmed.

"And at what point did you decide to go to Helen's?" Jake asked.

"I—well—" Ty stumbled over his words. "Sally and I got in an argument, so I left."

Sally glared at me. As if I was responsible for their problems. It wasn't my fault her boyfriend was a total flirt.

"And you went over to Helen's?" Jake asked.

Sally leaned forward slightly as if she didn't even know this part of the story.

"I was on my way to see PJ when I saw Helen walking up her driveway," Ty said. "That's when I called you."

"And I told you to stay back," Jake said.

"Right, but I didn't want her to get hurt. So, I followed her inside, but by the time I got there, she was already dead on the floor."

"And did you see PJ?"

"Yeah," Ty said. "He was standing over Helen with a knife in his hand."

"We found quite a bit of blood on his shirt," Jake said. "Did it look like he'd moved her body or tried to resuscitate her?"

"I don't know," Ty said, his words tired. "I was too busy worrying he was going to kill me next."

"So you pulled out a gun?" Jake asked.

"A gun?" Ty said. "Uh, no. The gun wasn't mine. It was PJ's."

"Okay, so PJ was holding a knife and a gun?"

Ty rubbed his head with the hand that had an IV sticking out of the back.

"Yeah, maybe," he said. "It happened really fast. He shot at me."

"How many times?"

"Four or five."

"And then he hit you?"

"Right in the leg," Ty said. "I thought he was going to end me when I fell on the floor, but instead, he put the gun to his chest and pulled the trigger."

It was so brutal, the whole thing. The buzzing in my hair slowed at the thought of it. Death was literally a buzzkill.

"Why do you think he killed Helen?" Jake asked.

"Because he wanted her land," Ty said. "We talked about it. But I didn't think he'd kill her. I didn't think he'd killed Uncle Percy. I thought Aunt Helen killed Uncle Percy when she found out he had a son."

"She's known about PJ," Hank said.

Jake nodded as if Hank had told him that story.

"But she didn't know about the will," Ty said.

"The will doesn't hold any weight," Hank said. "The farm was never Percy's to give away."

"Aunt Helen didn't sign the prenup," Ty said.

Hank looked over at Earl, who nodded.

"She didn't," Earl said. "But her case was solid. She still owned the land while she was alive."

"And now?" Hank asked.

Earl shook his head. "Now things are trickier. If PJ lives—"

"Wait, he's still alive?" Ty asked, his eyes wide. "How? He shot himself in the heart."

"He missed by centimeters," Hank said. "The doctors fixed him up, though his chance at survival is still low."

"So if he lives, he gets the farm?" Ty asked.

"Technically, yes," Earl said. "But we could still fight it."

"What if he dies?" Ty said.

"Then it would be up to the judge whether to keep the farm in the family or to give it to PJ's mother."

Ty looked like he was going to pass out. Hank did too.

"I cannot believe this," Hank said.

"Right now, we need to focus on getting Ty better," Sally said. "That's all that matters."

Ty closed his eyes. "Sally, why don't you go home."

"But Ty—"

"Just because I'm in the hospital does not change what happened last night. We're through."

Sally gasped. "But—"

"Go home," Ty said, more forcibly now.

"Come on," Katie said. "I'll walk you out."

Sally stormed past us. "I can walk myself out."

Once Sally was gone, Jake asked, "Is there anything else you can remember?"

"Not that I can think of."

Jake nodded and put his writing pad back in his pocket before turning to me. "Ellie, can I talk to you in the hallway?"

I was surprised he wanted to talk to me. But I agreed.

"Last night, do you remember hearing any gunshots?" he asked once we were safely in the corridor.

"I think I fell asleep pretty quickly," I said. "I didn't hear anything."

"And you were in Esme's room, right?"

I nodded. I mean, it wasn't a total lie. I was in a part of her room.

"Why did you lock the door?"

"I didn't," I said. "It must have locked on its own. It is an old house."

"Esme's house always acted up a bit." Jake laughed. "And did you get any feelings about any of this?"

I'd forgotten I was supposed to be trying to feel something.

I thought for a minute.

"I felt sad about all the violence," I said.

He nodded but waited for me to continue.

"Honestly," I said. "This sounds weird, but this doesn't seem to add up."

Jake smiled. "How so?"

"I don't know. There's just something off about it. Like, what if Helen killed Percy and then was going over to kill PJ? Maybe he acted in self-defense."

"Self-defense, huh?" This seemed to surprise him.

"Maybe?" I shrugged. "Probably not. Why? What do you think?"

"I'm not convinced PJ did all this—at least not alone."

"You think he had an accomplice?"

"I think it's interesting that he killed one person with a knife and then went after another with a gun."

"Especially since he hates guns," I said. "But who?"

"I think we should talk to that fiancée of his."

"Well, then, go ahead," a woman's voice said from behind us. "Ask me what you need so we can clear PJ's name."

2 1

I tried to be cognizant about my feelings while Jake questioned the beautiful woman in front of us, but I couldn't help compare every little thing about her to me. At least I had cooler hair. Even if I had to hide it most of the time.

Jake asked about the night before—she said she had been in Des Moines and had about fifteen people who could verify because she was at her Bachelorette Party.

"Do you think PJ had anything to do with Percy's murder?" Jake asked.

"No way," the woman said. "Percy sent him money every month. That's how he started his businesses in Des Moines and Chicago. The minute Percy died was the minute he knew he wouldn't get the money anymore."

"If that's the case," Jake asked. "Do you think he could be responsible for Helen's murder?"

She hesitated a bit on this one. "I don't think he'd be so desperate as to kill someone, even if he was having trouble coming up with money."

"What do you mean by that?" Jake asked gently.

"Some of the contractors have been irritated because he hasn't been able to pay them on time. He pays them," she added quickly. "It's just a little late sometimes."

"But he had enough money to pay Ty before Ty had even sold him the place," I said, then realized I was probably not supposed to ask questions. "Sorry."

Jake didn't respond, just nodded. "She has a point."

"PJ didn't give Ty that money," she said, shaking her cute little head.

"If PJ didn't, who did?" Jake asked.

"How am I supposed to know?" she looked down at her nails. "But it definitely wasn't PJ."

"Is there anyone else who might gain something by owning the two farms?" Jake asked.

She shrugged. "Maybe the board or the investors?"

"Investors?" Jake asked.

"Well, investor," she said. "His mom. She fronted him quite a bit of money to get the business started."

"PJ's mom?" Jake asked. "And where was she last night?"

"I don't keep up with that old witch," PJ's fiancée said. "If you want to talk to her, you'll have to find her yourself."

Jake said his thank-yous, and the woman returned to PJ's room.

"Any feelings?" Jake asked.

"I don't think she did it," I said.

"Neither do I," he replied.

I offered to get everyone lunch from a deli I'd seen a few blocks from the hospital. I needed the break. Hank went back and forth between arguing with Ty and consulting with Earl about the status of his family farm. From what I could tell, things weren't looking promising for Hank to keep the property.

And Ty was in a lot of trouble.

When I walked into the deli, the smell of freshly baked bread, sliced meats, and veggies made me salivate. As I approached the counter, I heard someone call my name.

I turned to find Sally sitting at a corner booth with tear streaks down her face.

"I suppose you don't want to talk to me," she said.

"I'll talk to you." I sat across from her. "Why wouldn't I want to talk to you?"

"Because you're with Ty now."

I laughed. "I am most certainly not with Ty now. I was on a date—or what I thought was a date—with PJ last night."

"I'm not stupid," Sally said. "I know Ty wasn't driving over to talk to PJ last night. He was going to check on you. The two of you were probably making out when you saw Helen."

I reached across the table and grabbed Sally's hand. "I didn't see Ty last night after the two of you dropped me off. I promise."

She seemed relieved. "You're just like her, you know?"

"Like Esme?" I asked. "I've been told."

"No—I mean—yes, like Esme. But I meant you're like Emily."

I swallowed. "You knew my mother?"

"We were best friends back in the day." Sally looked out the window at the people passing by. "The three of us were inseparable."

"The three of you?"

"Me, Jake, and Emily," she looked at me as if I should have known that. "I figured Jake told you."

"Jake told me he and Emily were merely acquaintances."

Sally tilted her head back and laughed. "That's hilarious. Just acquaintances, huh?"

I nodded, unable to speak and thankful my hood was still up.

"That's surprising, though, I'm sure it's because of, well, you know."

"Because of what?" I asked.

"Jake and Emily ended up together," Sally said, her voice turning bitter. "They broke up our little group. I was left out while they kissed and held hands. I was nothing. But when your mother up and left, he came running to me. Fancy that."

"Did you know?"

"That she was pregnant?" She shook her head. "No one did."

"Have you seen her since?"

"Nope. It was almost like she just disappeared."

"And—" my voice caught in my throat. I wanted to ask, but I didn't know how. I couldn't.

"And?" She seemed to know what I was struggling to ask.

"Was—is—Jake my father?" I asked.

"It would seem that way, wouldn't it?" she said.

I sat back in my chair, letting go of her hand.

Why had he lied to me?

"But even though you both have the same eyes, I don't know that he's the man you're looking for."

"What? Why not?"

"Because Jake and your mother never—" she raised her eyebrows up and down "—you know."

"Oh," I said, disappointment flowing through every last hair follicle.

"Yours does it too, huh?" Sally said, hooking a finger around a loose curl that had escaped the hoodie.

"Does everyone know?" I asked.

"Everyone in town," Sally said. "It's no big deal, though."

"Did Emily's change?"

"Her hair?" Sally laughed. "Her hair changed so much, we didn't know what its original form was."

"If Jake isn't my father," I said. "Do you know who is?"

"Couldn't say," Sally said. "Maybe no one. I mean, she was a witch after all." Sally winked and stood. "Good talk. I'm glad you're not with Ty."

I was so flustered by her abruptness, I didn't ask her any other questions.

By the end of the day, Ty was released and home with his parents. PJ was still in his hospital bed with his fiancée at his bedside. I didn't get home until after dark. The moon was full and shining bright over the cleared field.

I hopped out of Jake's truck, emotionally exhausted.

"Hey, Ellie?" Jake said before I closed the door.

I turned back and looked up at him. "Yeah?"

"Is everything okay? You haven't said five words since lunch."

"Everything is fine." I didn't have it in me to confront him knowing he knew my mother. "I'm just tired."

"Okay," he said. "Thanks for your help today."

"I didn't really help," I said. "I don't get the feelings like Esme did."

"I think you'll get there."

I shrugged. I didn't care at this point whether I'd get there or not. My hair was not magical. It just changed color every once in a while. It was a nuisance.

"Have a good night," he said.

"You too." I closed the door and let myself into the house. Penelope was waiting with her sparkly leash in her mouth.

"A walk? Now?"

She oinked excitedly.

"But I'm tired."

She oinked again.

"Okay, but just a short one. Then we're going to bed."

When we got to the end of the driveway, Penelope led me toward Helen and Percy's place. As we approached, I felt an overwhelming sense of sadness mixed with expectation.

We walked up the driveway to find the side door standing wide open.

"We shouldn't go in," I said down to Penelope. "It's a crime scene."

Penelope tugged at the leash.

"No," I said more forcefully, even though I had the same draw to go inside and see things for myself.

But Penelope would not stop tugging. She dug her heels in and wouldn't give up.

Finally, I reached down to scoop her up, but somehow when I did, the latch on the leash came free, and Penelope jumped away from me and dashed into Helen's house.

I peeked in the door. "Penelope, get out here."

No response.

I couldn't even hear her footsteps.

"Pen-el-o-pe," I enunciated each syllable. She'd never done this before. "I cannot come inside. It is a crime scene. Get out of there."

Nothing.

I pulled out my phone, which—yes—I was carrying because Katie had begged me to keep it with me in case they needed to get in touch.

"Jake?" I said when he answered.

"Ellie," he said. "Are you okay? What's wrong?"

"Penelope and I took a walk, and the door of Percy and Helen's house was open, and she darted inside. Should I go in and get her? I don't want to disturb the crime scene."

"Smart girl." I could hear the smile in his voice. "I'll be right there, and we can get her together."

I paced by the door, occasionally shouting for Penelope to come out until Jake pulled in.

"Still hasn't come out?"

I shook my head.

"Okay, follow me. But know, there might still be blood and other things that haven't been cleaned up."

I followed, trying to keep my eyes off anything that might freak me out. My scalp was already tingling.

"You know those feelings Esme used to get?" I asked.

"Yes."

"Did she ever explain them to you?" I looked around, but there was no sign of Penelope. "Like how they felt or anything?"

"Not really," Jake said. "Why?"

"I think I had one that led me here. I think Penelope might have too."

"Penelope?" Jake looked at me like I was crazy.

"I don't know. It was weird. It was like there was some strange pull dragging us both up the driveway to the house."

"That is weird."

The time to avert my eyes was when we got to the living room. But I couldn't do it. There was way too much going on. Blood soaked into the hardwood floor was likely from Helen. An upholstered chair had blood on it also. Maybe that was where PJ had shot himself?

"Do you see her?" I asked. "Penelope?"

"No," Jake said. "I'll check the back."

I looked under the table and around the furniture in the living room. Penelope was nowhere to be found.

As I left the room, my hair buzzed as if I'd sucked

down a triple shot latte. I turned around and tried to feel for what my hair might be telling me. Was it telling me anything? Or was I just reading too much into it? Wanting it to happen?

I approached the wall across from where the upholstered chair sat with PJ's blood on it. "What?" I mumbled. "What do I need to see?"

I looked around. Up and down. The popcorn ceiling was covered in dust but nothing more. The floor here was normal besides a speck of blood marked by a little yellow tag with a number on it.

I bent down to examine the floor. Right next to the bloodstain was a table where a pile of mail had accumulated. My hair buzzed more. I dropped to my knees.

I glanced under the table to find a shell casing and what looked like a bullet hole going straight into the floor.

"Jake?" I called.

"Still haven't found her," he said. "Are you sure she came in here?" He emerged from the back of the house. "Why are you on the floor?"

"I think I found something that the forensic people may have missed?" I glanced around. Little yellow tags were all over the room, marking places that seemed to be evidence, but no tags indicated anything was under the table.

"What is it?" He got down on the floor and peeked under the table.

"I think it's a shell casing and maybe a bullet hole?"

"A bullet hole in the floor?" He pulled on a pair of gloves and ran his finger over the hole. "It sure looks like it."

"Maybe it was one of the stray bullets PJ shot at Ty?"

"This is where we found Ty with a bullet through his leg." He pointed to the blood. "This is from his wound."

"If Ty walked in after PJ killed Helen—" I always did my best thinking when I thought aloud "—why wouldn't PJ have tried to stab Ty too? Where did the gun come from?"

"We think the gun came from Helen," Jake said.

"So, you agree she might have come over here to kill PJ?" I looked around. "But if she had the gun, how did Ty and PJ get shot? She couldn't have shot them after she was stabbed, could she?"

"We found the gun in PJ's left hand. Maybe he got it away from her and then stabbed her." Jake said. "You said PJ didn't like guns, right?"

"But then he shot Ty and himself?" It made no sense.

"I'll get the forensics guys back over to collect the evidence," Jake said. "Maybe we can figure out more with additional evidence."

An oink came from behind me. Penelope emerged from the other side of the couch—where I'd just looked for her. "Where were you hiding?"

She was back to her usual cuddly self. She nuzzled me with her wiggly nose in apology.

"It's all right," I said. "But next time, do not run into a crime scene."

"Speaking of crime scene," a woman said at the door. "Can I come in?"

Jake stood quickly, putting himself between the woman and me. "Why would you need to come in?"

"Because I am the new owner of this house," she said. "I'm Bonnie Carter, PJ's mother."

I peeked around Jake to find a gorgeous and smug-looking woman. She wore black leggings, a crisp white button-down shirt, and a puffy black vest over top. Her hair was salt and pepper gray, and she had the same smile as PJ.

She was the woman I'd seen on the news my first night in Esme's house. The developer.

"I'm sorry, Ms. Carter," Jake said. "I can't allow anyone on the premises."

"Then why is she here?" Bonnie said.

"She's assisting," Jake said.

"With a pig?" Bonnie laughed. "What kind of Podunk town is this?"

Jake puffed up his chest. "Ma'am, you may not be here. We can set you up in a hotel room a couple of towns down if that would suit you."

"I can find my own place to stay," she said.

"Why aren't you at the hospital with PJ?" I asked.

She sneered. "He has the woman of his life with him. He doesn't need his poor mother anymore."

"I'm sure he'd love for you to be there. He used to always talk about how amazing you were, raising him as a single mother."

She narrowed her eyes. "And who are you?"

"Oh, sorry." I stepped out from behind Jake. "I'm Ellie Vanderwick. And this is Penelope."

She didn't even glance at Penelope.

"I dated PJ when I lived in Colorado," I said.

She looked confused. Then it was like a lightbulb

turned on in her head. "You're the one with the hair, right?"

He'd talked about me?

"Uh, I guess," I said.

"PJ thought you were the one until your little secret came out."

"My secret?"

"Your magnificent color-changing hair." She pulled out her phone and glanced at it for a split second before returning it to her sleek black purse.

I sighed.

"Either way," Jake said. "You should probably get to the hospital. I hear PJ isn't doing well."

"He's not," she said. "He's dead."

Dead? I sucked in a breath.

"How do you—" Jake said, but she cut him off.

"Just got a text from the fiancée. He's dead." She looked like she might be in shock. "Looks like she won't get her hands on his fortune after all." The laugh that came out of her mouth sounded other-worldly. Penelope tucked her head into my armpit.

"His fortune?" Jake asked. "His fiancée said he was broke. Having a hard time paying people."

"She doesn't know what she's talking about," Bonnie waved a hand in the air. "Please phone me when all of this is cleaned up." She walked away without another word.

"How do you feel about living next to a housing development?" Jake asked.

"I don't think I have a choice in the matter."

I slept well into the morning the next day and only woke up because my stomach was grumbling. It was Thursday—my day off—and I was planning on doing absolutely nothing.

But it always seemed like when I made plans, they didn't quite work out the way I expected.

As I poured myself a bowl of cereal from the nearly empty box, a knock came at the door.

Penelope trotted out ahead of me and waited for me to answer.

I pulled the door open to find Ty standing on my steps.

"Oh my goodness," I said. "Are you supposed to be out and about?"

"The doctor probably wouldn't approve, but I can't just lay in bed all day." He walked with the help of crutches.

"Come sit down," I said. "Can I get you anything? I don't have much, but I have some cereal and water."

"I'm okay," he said. "I just wanted to make sure you

were okay. I didn't get to talk to you at the hospital with all the craziness going on."

"You came over to check on me?" I asked. "In your condition?"

"Esme would have wanted me to," he said. "I've been thinking about all of this the wrong way. I think it was Sally's influence. She and I had been together so long, and she was older, and I was just used to doing what I could to make her happy."

"The diamonds?"

Ty nodded. "But those were fake. I didn't have nearly enough money to buy her what she really wanted."

"She never suspected?"

"Maybe she didn't want to know." He shrugged. "I think she was only with me because I stood to inherit three farms and could have made a lot of money off them. She's the one who initially contacted PJ's company, after all."

"Three farms?"

"Ours, Percy's, and Esme's."

"Right," I said. "I forgot about Esme's."

"Speaking of, have you filed the paperwork that needed to be filed?"

My mind went to the papers upstairs. "I haven't even looked through the documents. I'm going to wait until I can afford a lawyer to do anything with them."

"So, you haven't?"

Maybe he was still loopy from pain medication. "Not yet."

Ty's face contorted from sweet to something else. Something that made my scalp burn. "I guess it's time I told you, you have twenty-four hours to pack up and leave."

I knew my hair was turning bright red, but Ty didn't seem to mind. "What do you mean I have to pack up and leave?"

"In the paperwork, Esme specifically said if you didn't accept the inheritance by yesterday, you would forfeit it to me."

"But—"

"No buts." He shook his head and gave me a mock pouty face. "Esme loved me. I was more of a grandchild to her than you will ever be. She didn't want to wait for you forever when she knew I was here and could take over the farm. So she set a limitation for you to claim it—six months."

My heart dropped. I raced upstairs to retrieve the paperwork. I needed to get Earl over to look at it. Why hadn't I considered talking to him the minute I found out he was an attorney?

The pages were scattered all over the attic where I'd hastily left them. I tried to arrange them into order before I ran back down to Esme's bedroom and closed the secret door just before Ty peeked in.

"Need some help?" Ty leaned against the door frame. "I put the papers together, after all."

"You put the papers together?" I stood. "But you're not an attorney."

"I didn't prepare the paperwork. I just arranged them and sent them to you."

I looked at the original address more closely. It looked similar to a place I'd lived with a couple of other waitresses until I'd gotten fired. But the numbers were wrong. "Where did you get the address to send it to?"

"Esme found it," Ty said. "Once she knew you existed, it only took her a few days to figure out where you were."

"But this isn't the right address," I said. "The numbers are wrong. And the street name is too. It wasn't Bluebird Hill. It was Bluebird Lane."

"That was probably my fault." Ty shrugged.

It was a wonder the package had found me at all.

"How did Esme find out about me?" I shuffled through the papers again, looking for where it said I only had six months.

"She never told me how she found you." He glanced at the papers in my hands. "Want me to show you?"

I pulled them to my chest.

"Fine," he said. "Page twelve."

I flipped through, but the pages weren't in order. It took me a few minutes to go through the page numbers and find the number twelve.

"Bottom paragraph."

I read a paragraph I didn't understand completely, but it did say something about claiming the property within six months, or it would go to Ty.

"Now you know." Ty didn't look apologetic at all. In fact, he looked like he'd just won the lottery. Which he practically had.

Tears sprung to my eyes, and my hair fell limp down my back. "I'll pack my things and be out by tomorrow morning." It would be okay. I still had Mona and Penelope.

"No hard feelings, though, right?" Ty said.

I took a breath. "No," I answered. "It was what Esme wanted."

"Do you think you'll stay in town?"

I shrugged.

"Well, if you do, I'd love to take you out to dinner sometime."

I couldn't believe he was asking me out after he'd practically shoved my nose in the mud in defeat.

"I'll get out of your hair then," Ty said, hobbling down the steps. "Thanks for taking care of the house for me."

I wanted to throw something at him, but that wasn't fair. If Esme loved him like a grandson, he deserved at least a bit of kindness. After all, I'd be pretty bummed if I was in his shoes—taking care of Esme and the farm—only to find out she had a biological granddaughter who would inherit everything that was rightfully his.

It was probably better this way.

"Let's go up to the attic one more time," I said to Penelope.

Esme's journal was still on the stand next to the chair. I hadn't gotten up the courage to read it. What if she wasn't the wonderful person I'd created in my mind? What if she talked about Emily in a way I couldn't handle?

Instead of reading it, I clutched it to my chest, wrapped up in a blanket, and sat in the sun for what felt like hours.

2 4

When I finally re-emerged to the main level, I decided I'd better start packing. It wasn't like I had much, but it would be easy to lose things in a house this big. Plus, I still needed to clean Dewdrop. I wouldn't want Ty moving back in and thinking I was a total slob for not picking up his room. Then I'd need to take Katie her clothes.

Big Bertha was packed within minutes—my packing skills were something I didn't think I'd ever have to use again. But what good was a skill if you didn't use it? I smiled at the thought. There was no use crying over what could have been. I'd learned that a long time ago.

I found some cleaner, gloves, and a rag in one of the bathroom closets and went to work getting everything sparkling clean. The bathroom I'd been using in Borealis wasn't hard. I'd barely been there a week.

I set the spray bottle down.

Wow.

Had it really only been a week?

It was funny how I felt so at home in such a small amount of time. Maybe I really would stay. I mean, I'd have to live in Mona for a while until I could afford a place, but eventually, I might rent one of the cute apartments in town over the shops or something.

I made my way to Dewdrop to find it messier than I remembered. The bed had the silky comforter pulled up, but the sheets underneath were in a big ball. I stripped the bed and went searching for an extra set of sheets.

I made the bed and stood back to admire my handy work. The room looked and smelled much nicer. I gathered up the dirty sheets and took them down the hall to the laundry area. In front of the washer was a heap of clothes. I picked up one piece of clothing to find a holy t-shirt that smelled horrible. I dropped it back into the pile. Those could be dealt with at a later time.

I put the sheets into the washer and heard a clinking sound. Something had fallen out of them. I carefully pulled the sheets from the washer and piled them on the floor next to the towels. Inside the silver drum was a gold ring like the one Earl and the other farmers wore. It had a symbol on it that looked like a three-pronged trident.

I slipped the ring in my pocket and put the sheets back into the washer.

Once the washer was going, I decided I'd drop off Katie's things and then take Ty his ring. If all the farmers wore them, it was probably pretty special.

When I pulled up in Katie's driveway, Mona sputtered to a halt. She barely started as if she knew we were moving. Silly van. She was probably just bummed that she wouldn't be spending the winter in a warm cozy garage.

"I wasn't expecting to see you this afternoon," Katie said, opening the door for me to come in.

"I just wanted to bring your things back," I said. "Thank you for letting me borrow them."

"Sweetie, you can keep them. My daughter left a whole closet full of clothes. Do you want to come see them?"

Giddiness rose inside me.

"I'll take that as a yes." Katie pointed to my hair.

I looked in a mirror to find my hair a bright bubble gum pink. It was a little disconcerting that I hadn't even felt it change.

"Come on," Katie said, leading me up the stairs.

Their daughter's bedroom was absolutely gorgeous. It had the same flair as the rest of the house—very artistic—but slightly more leaning toward the performing arts with posters of Broadway musicals and movie ticket stubs. "Did she see all these shows?"

Katie nodded. "We used to go to New York a lot. Melody was incredibly talented in the performing arts, and I wanted to nurture that in her. That's why I started the local theater."

"You started a theater?" I asked.

Katie blushed. "It's more of a hobby than anything, but we put on a couple of shows a year." Katie picked up a photo of her with a girl who could have been her clone if they were the same age. "You'll have to come see the Christmas show. It's always a town favorite."

"Yeah, maybe." I didn't want to commit to something when I didn't know if I'd even be there for Christmas.

Katie opened the closet doors revealing a huge, perfectly organized walk-in closet. Shoes each had their own clear plastic containers, Purses either hung or were displayed on shelves. And the clothes. My head spun. There were more clothes than I'd ever seen in anyone's closet.

A pang of jealousy raced through me faster than I could stop it. Katie and Earl were the perfect parents. Melody was a lucky girl. And I was just a fill-in. The girl they'd dump the minute Melody returned.

"Are you okay?" Katie asked.

"I'm sorry," I said. "I don't think I should do this."

"What are you going on about?"

"It's just—I don't want you to do something just because you miss Melody. And I don't want to be—"

"A replacement?" Katie asked.

I glanced up at her. "How did you know?"

"Ellie Vanderwick." She held my hands in hers. "You could never be a replacement for our Melody. But you can be a special part of our lives. You deserve a family just as much as any of us."

Emotion flooded my heart.

"Now, you can take whatever you want," Katie said in a matter-of-fact tone. "Well, other than the costumes in the back corner and the dresses on that side—those were from her formal dances, and I'd like to keep them. But anything else, shoes, handbags, whatever, go right ahead."

I didn't even know where to start.

"How about I get a couple of totes, and we can pack it up for you? Melody told me a long time ago to donate all of it to charity. She has fancy Hollywood clothes now." Katie rolled her eyes a bit, but it was in more of a teasing manner.

She disappeared from the room as I gazed around. There were stacks of jeans in every color, skirts that still had the tags on them, blouses and jackets and tank tops. My mind was exploding. Katie was going to give me all of this?

Then excitement was replaced with disappointment. Where would I put it all? I was going to live in Mona for who knew how long. This closet was at least twice the size of the van's living quarters.

Katie came back with several totes but stopped short when she saw the look on my face. "What's wrong?"

"I-I can't take all of this." I tried to keep emotion from my voice, but one look in the mirror showed that my hair didn't care to hide its feelings. A greenish-blue had replaced the pink.

"Sure you can," Katie said. "I'd be so happy to see it get used."

I shook my head. "It's not that I don't want to," I said. "It's that I don't know where I'd put it."

Katie looked confused. "You have about fifteen bedrooms, and Esme's closet is one of legends."

I'd never even looked inside Esme's closet. Sadness overtook me. I'd never get to explore the house, discover its secrets, sit in Esme's closet soaking up the way she smelled.

"What is it?" Katie asked, wiping a lone tear from my cheek.

"The house doesn't belong to me anymore," I said. "I'm going to live in my van—Mona."

"What do you mean the house doesn't belong to you?" Katie asked. "You didn't sell it, did you?"

"Oh no," I said. "Nothing like that. It's just I didn't follow through with filing the paperwork when I got here, and since it's been over six months, the house belongs to Ty."

Katie's mouth dropped open.

"It's really okay." Maybe if I said that over and over again, it would be. "Ty deserves it."

"Ty absolutely does not deserve it. It's rightfully yours. Esme wanted you to have it."

"But before she wanted me to have it, she wanted Ty to have it." I sighed. "If she hadn't ever found out about me, this wouldn't even be an issue."

Katie laid a hand on my shoulder. "There's so much you still don't know."

"Either way. It's written in the contract that if I didn't claim the property in time, it would be Ty's."

"A technicality," Katie said. "I'll get Earl on it right away and—"

I grabbed her hand. "It's okay." I glanced into the closet. "But maybe I could take a few of the warmer things? It might get pretty cold in the van over the winter."

"You will not live in a van," Katie said. "You will live here. If Earl can't get this worked out, you'll move in with us. We have an extra room. The closet's not this nice, but it's something."

"You're so sweet," I said. "But I couldn't impose. I've lived in the van more than I've lived in a house. She's been my home since I could drive."

"But you're not leaving town, right?" Katie asked.

I shook my head. "No. I think I'll stick around a while."

Katie brushed away a tear. "Good. That's good." She looked at all the clothes. "Well then, let's get all the warmest clothes."

Once we'd settled on an appropriate amount of clothes, I thanked her and said goodbye.

Mona grumbled to a start when I turned the key in the ignition. "Come on, aren't you happy that Penelope and I will live with you again?"

She sputtered.

I hugged the steering wheel. "You're my home."

The engine quieted to a warm hum as we made our way to Hank and Nancy's to return Ty's ring.

The house was dark, besides one light coming from what I assumed was the kitchen because it had little herb pots in the window. It wasn't that late, but I knew farmers liked to go to bed early so they could get a fresh start on the day.

I knocked gently on the door in case anyone was sleeping. I didn't want to wake anyone, but that plan was thwarted when I heard what sounded like an entire herd of dogs on the other side of the door barking and clawing.

"Shut up," a woman's voice yelled from inside.

The door opened a crack so as not to let the dogs out. Sally's face and two little corgi snouts peeked out.

"Oh, hi," I said. "I didn't expect to see you here."

"No?" Sally said. "Ty and I were just hanging out."

"Great." I shifted from one foot to another.

The dogs were still going crazy on the other side of the door.

"Knock it off," she yelled down at them, but it didn't have the desired effect. "What do you need?"

"Oh, right," I said. "I just came to return this." I pulled the ring from my pocket. "I think it was Ty's. It was in the sheets on his bed. I found it when I was doing laundry."

She snatched the ring from my hand. "I told you once, and I'll tell you again. Stay. Away. From. Ty."

"I was—I just wanted to bring—"

But she slammed the door in my face.

The dogs quieted when I backed away from the door.

I turned to go back to Mona, but my hair buzzed again like it had when I was near Helen's house.

Something was wrong.

I tip-toed to look in a window but found nothing. It was too dark.

The kitchen window was too high to look inside, but it was the only one with light.

I glanced around to find something I might be able to stand on.

A rock big enough for me to reach the window would be too heavy for me to move. I looked around for something else until my gaze landed on two Adirondack chairs sitting next to a metal fire pit.

That would work.

At first, it seemed like the chair was cemented to the ground. Who knew it would be so heavy?

I finally got it moving and placed under the window with the herb pots.

I pulled the hood of my hoodie up over my hair just in case it started changing so it wouldn't give me away. Then I peeked inside the window.

I could barely see anything from standing on the seat, so I stepped up onto the arms.

From that vantage point, I could see everything. And seeing everything made my scalp burn and my stomach drop.

Sally stood with her back to me, holding a kitchen knife in her hand, while Nancy and Hank were tied to chairs.

My brain hurt. Did Sally kill Percy? And what about Helen and PJ and Ty?

Hank saw me and shook his head slightly as if to tell me to get away. But no part of me would let Sally stab another one of my friends.

I could hear Sally ranting through the thin glass of the window.

"Ty deserves this farm," she said. "He's worked so hard for all of you, and all he gets is a bullet through the leg. First, he lost out on Esme's place—"

Apparently, she hadn't spoken to Ty recently.

"Then Helen's and now you won't even let him have what's rightfully his."

Neither of them replied.

"But if you're gone, then Ty can have the farm," she said. "And he'll love me again because I got it for him."

"You think he's going to love you for killing his parents?" Nancy said. She wore bright red pajamas that brought out the extra rosiness in her cheeks. "When he finds out you killed his aunt and uncle, he's never going to speak to you again."

Sally approached Nancy.

I needed to do something. Sally was going to stab her.

I pulled out my phone and hit Jake's contact.

"Hello?" Jake said.

I ducked down and turned my face away from the house. "Jake, I need you at Hank's right now. Sally's got Hank and Nancy tied up, and she's going to stab them."

"Stay safe," Jake said. "I'll be right there."

I shut off my phone and stood back up.

Nancy was still alive, but Sally was standing over her, whispering something that made Nancy's eyes widen.

Sally took a step back and then raised the knife.

"No!" I yelled.

All I saw was Sally turn before I toppled over backward into a rose bush. Thorns tore at my clothes and poked through my yoga pants.

I heard the door I'd just been at open and then close.

I had to get away from the window. If Sally found me, I'd end up just like Hank and Nancy.

I waited to hear from which direction she was approaching. Then tore off the other way. If there was one thing about me, I was fast. Maybe not as fast as Helen was, but there was no way Sally would beat me in a foot race.

But getting away wasn't the plan. I couldn't leave Hank and Nancy.

Instead, I circled back around to the door, opened it, and went inside. I locked it behind me.

When I got to the kitchen, Nancy let out a sob.

"Oh, thank God," Hank said.

I moved to untie them, but Hank stopped me. "No time. You need to lock the rest of the doors."

I glanced around. I didn't see any other doors.

"Where are they?"

"Down the hall and to the left is one, and then take the stairs to the basement and lock the walk-out door."

I took off, the dogs barking and chasing after me. Corgis were herding dogs, and my ankles felt their wrath.

Hank yelled for the dogs to come back, and they obeyed immediately.

I got to the first door in time and then made my way down the old farmhouse stairs as quickly as I could without tumbling.

The basement was pitch black, but I could make out shapes. I didn't want to turn on a light and alert Sally to where I was.

I stepped carefully around what felt like a couch and found the wall. I walked around, feeling for a door. I tried to control my breathing and not think about how tight the space felt in the dark. Since one of my foster siblings had trapped me in a closet during a vicious game of hide and seek, I occasionally froze up when I felt claustrophobic.

When my hand came to rest on a doorknob, it began to turn. I quickly flipped the lock and felt for a deadbolt. I flipped that too and then hurried back toward the stairs as quickly as I could without tripping over anything. When I re-emerged into the light, my heart rate slowed.

Sally had been on the other side of that door.

But I'd stopped her.

I ran back upstairs, taking them two at a time, but when I came to the kitchen, my heart practically stopped.

Sally was standing with a smile on her face and a knife in her hand.

26

"Sit down," she sneered. "If you want to live."

"How did you—"

"Ty's window," she said. "I've snuck in a time or two. It's almost poetic. Because the two of you are such prudes and wouldn't let your *adult* son have his girlfriend spend the night, he found a way to sneak her in. Then, as you're trying to keep her out again, she comes back through the window. It's like Ty gave me access so I could do this all along."

"I don't think killing his parents was what was on Ty's mind when he let you in his window," Hank said, his voice full of disapproval.

"Either way," Sally said with an evil laugh and a shrug. "Sit down," she yelled at me.

I took a seat on one of the bar stools at the kitchen island.

"Don't move."

I nodded. I wasn't about to be the reason she killed Hank or Nancy.

My mind went to Jake. Was that who was trying to get into the basement? Had I locked out the only person who knew we were here? The only person who could save us?

"Look," Hank said. "Just let us go. We won't press charges. We'll give Ty the farm."

"No," Nancy said. "We're not giving him the farm. He doesn't deserve it."

"How could you say that?" Sally said. "Ty does everything around here."

"Oh, Sally," Nancy said, shaking her head. "You've been blinded by love. Ty is not worth killing someone over. No one is."

Sally seemed to falter in her decision.

I glanced around the island for something—anything—I could use to defend myself and my friends, but the only things there were a basket of fruit and what looked like Ty's bag of personal effects from the hospital, including the god-awful brown and green paisley shirt.

If I couldn't find something to overpower her with, I'd have to go with whatever bit of cleverness I could come up with.

"Sally," I said, an idea popping into my head. "I know we're not friends, but you were once friends with my mother."

Hank and Nancy both looked at me wide-eyed as if they were surprised I knew this information.

"And if you were friends with my mother, it was because you were a good person." I shifted my butt on the stool. It was still tender from falling in the rose bush. "And I'd venture to guess you still are a good person."

Sally dropped the knife a fraction of an inch.

"There are so many men in the world. Men better than Ty." I turned to Nancy and Hank. "No offense."

"None taken," Hank said.

"You can find someone who treats you with kindness and respect. Who doesn't buy you fake jewelry."

"Fake?" Sally looked down at the diamond bracelet on her wrist. "No. You're lying."

"I'm not," I said. "Ty told me tonight."

She set the knife down on the counter and took the bracelet off.

It was now or never.

I grabbed the knife and stood. "Don't move."

Sally froze, her eyes still on the bracelet.

Jake took this opportunity to barge through the front door. Keys dangled from the handle. "Stay where you are." He pointed his gun toward Sally.

"Don't shoot me," she said. "I did nothing wrong."

"You killed my Aunt and Uncle," Ty said, hobbling in from the hall that led to the bedrooms. He had apparently come through his window too. "And shot me and PJ."

Her eyes widened. "I did not."

"Yes, you did," Ty said. "I tried to protect you, but I can't do it anymore. You were going to kill my parents."

She glanced at the knife in my hand.

"What? No, I—" She looked from the gun then back to Ty. "I was doing it for us. This farm should be yours."

Ty shrugged. "There is no us. There will never be an us ever again."

Sally dropped her arms, letting the fake bracelet fall to the floor.

Jake snapped cuffs around her wrists and began reading her rights.

Ty and I worked together to untie his parents while Jake escorted Sally to his police car.

"Thank you so much," Nancy said to me. "You were so brave."

Hank wrapped me in a tight hug. "I'm glad you're here, kiddo."

"She won't be staying long," Ty said.

Hank pulled back and looked at me, his hands on my shoulders. "What is he talking about?"

I sucked in a breath. This had probably been the worst day I'd had in a long time. "The house rightfully belongs to Ty," I said. "But I won't leave town. Not right away, anyway. I kinda like it here."

Hank didn't smile. No one did.

"You're staying?" Ty asked. "Where are you going to live?"

I knew Ty wanted Esme's property. I didn't know he wanted me completely out of town.

"I'll live where I've lived most of my adult life," I said. "In my van—Mona."

Hank and Nancy exchanged a look.

"Don't even think about offering me a place to stay," I said before they did. "Katie already did. But I'll be fine."

"It gets pretty cold in the winter here," Hank said. "You'll freeze to death in a van."

"It got cold in the Colorado Rockies too." I smiled. "Mona's insulated, and I have a heater. It stays nice and toasty."

Ty huffed.

"Do you have a problem with me staying?" I asked him.

Ty's eyes widened as if he didn't expect me to call him out on his childish behavior. "It's just—" He hesitated. "It's just that you remind me of Esme, and I miss her so much. It's hard to even look at you sometimes."

"That's understandable," I said. "I'm happy to steer clear for a while so you can heal. But I'm not leaving town. I want to learn about my family. About Esme and Emily and . . ." I let the thought trail off. I'd wanted to say my father, but that might have been asking too much.

"I'm so sorry about this," Jake said, coming back through the door. "Are you all okay?"

"We're okay," Nancy said. "She wouldn't hurt us. She doesn't have it in her."

"She killed Uncle Percy and Aunt Helen and PJ, and she shot me," Ty practically shouted. "She's insane."

"Speaking of all that," Jake said. "I could also arrest you, Ty."

"For what?" Ty's eyes widened.

"For lying to a police officer," Jake said. "You told me that PJ killed Helen, Percy, and shot you and himself."

"I was just—"

"Protecting Sally?" Jake said. "I understand the need to protect someone you care about, but I'll need you to come down to the station and give me a corrected statement. I don't want to arrest you, but if you lie to me again, I will."

Ty nodded.

"Come on down tomorrow morning," Jake said. "I'll be busy with paperwork tonight."

"If it's okay with all of you," I said. "I'm going to go spend one last night in my grandmother's home."

Hank and Nancy looked like they wanted to say something, but Ty gave them the evil eye, and they kept their mouths shut.

Mona started right up, and we got back to the house just in time to find Penelope waiting for us on the porch.

"Why are you waiting out here?" I reached down to rub behind her ears, but she took off running like she needed to show me something.

27

"Wait up." I jogged behind her out to the barn. I'd never gone into the barn before. I always thought I'd get around to it, but never did.

When I walked in, it was as dark as a moonless night.

I reached around for a switch to turn on a light but found nothing.

"Hold on," I said, pulling out my phone. "I think this thing has a flashlight on it."

I swiped through the apps that came on the phone. I didn't have much use for any other apps. Having social media would mean I had friends—which I didn't until now. But I doubted Nancy and Katie were on social media.

Finally, I found the flashlight function and pointed it to the ground where Penelope stood waiting.

"Okay, show me," I said.

She trotted to the back of the barn. The floor underneath was soft from straw covering the dirt. It smelled like any barn, minus any animal feces.

When she stopped at the back wall, I waited.

"Now what?"

She oinked and tilted her head back.

I knew pigs were smart, but sometimes I felt like Penelope was exceptionally gifted.

I shone the flashlight beam coming from the back of my phone on the wall to find a painted mural. As I moved the beam around, the picture started to make sense. It was a farm—Esme's farm—with the house in its glory days, the barn, and people. I focused more closely on the people in the mural.

Three women with white hair stood side by side, facing away, looking at the house. My breath caught in my chest. I searched for more detail, something that might give me an insight into what it meant. A name had been signed in the bottom right corner of the mural.

Emily Vanderwick.

My mother had painted this. My mother.

I went back to the three women and ran a finger over them. My hair buzzed when I touched the final person. The youngest-looking of the three. This was supposed to be us—the three of us—Esme, Emily, and me.

But if this was here, why hadn't Esme thought to look for me? It very clearly showed three generations, and Esme had built the house.

I wanted to take a picture, but it was too dark. Every time I did, it ended up being all washed out from the flash on my phone.

I made a note in my mind to come back in the morning to get a photo.

"Let's go inside, Penelope. We have one more night to

enjoy Esme's house. We might as well make the most of it."

———

I slept in Esme's bed that night. From what I suspected, it would have been what she wanted in the first place. The feeling of comfort and warmth that encased me within the soft sheets and handmade quilts was something I'd hide away in the back of my mind for days when I felt cold and lonely.

Esme's bed was the only one in the house I had been able to sleep in. And now, I had to leave.

In the middle of the night, I shot up in bed. My hair was humming. Literally humming out loud.

I'd dreamed about something I couldn't quite grasp, but I knew it was important. It was about the murders.

Sally didn't do it.

I knew it like I knew my name. Sally did not kill anyone. And she wouldn't have killed Hank and Nancy.

But if Sally didn't do it, who did? That was what I wasn't able to get.

Were Esme's feelings like this?

I paced the room until daylight, lost in thought.

Percy and Helen had been poisoned, but Percy had died of stabbing. The knife that killed Percy ended up in Helen's house.

Helen had also died of stabbing with a knife similar to the one Percy was killed with. PJ and Ty had been shot. PJ in the chest and Ty in the leg.

If Percy and Helen died, PJ would get the farm since Helen hadn't signed the prenup. And if PJ died—

I gasped.

She couldn't have possibly killed her own son, could she?

I needed to find out.

Jake didn't answer his phone when I tried to call him. He was probably sleeping after the night he had. Or maybe he was interrogating Sally. Or talking to Ty.

I left a message for him to call me and hung up.

When I walked outside, the air was colder than it had been. The wind blew across the fields with enough force to knock someone over. I ran to Mona and pulled on a jacket Katie had given me.

If I was lucky, Bex could tell me where Bonnie was staying. I drove to the diner as the wind tried to topple Mona over. I'd called Bex the night before and let her know I had to tie up some loose ends this morning. She told me to just come in Saturday.

"It's freezing out there," I said when I walked in.

Bex smiled. "That's nothing," she said. "Wait until it's below zero and windy."

Maybe staying in Mona would be more challenging than I thought. I squared my shoulders. Nope, it would be fine. I could figure it out.

"Are you here to work or eat?" Bex asked.

"Neither," I said, staying as close to the door as I could so the farmers wouldn't see me. I didn't have time to engage in their conversations. "I need to ask you a question."

"Go ahead," she said.

"Do you know where Bonnie—PJ's mom—is staying in town?"

Bex frowned. "The past couple of weeks, she stayed at the little inn around the corner." She pointed behind her. "But now she's staying at Helen's house. Apparently, she owns it."

"But the police told her she couldn't because it was a crime scene."

"Was," Bex said. "It's not anymore. They cleared out when they discovered PJ did it."

"PJ didn't do it," I said.

"Oh, I heard," Bex said. "Sally did."

I shook my head. "Sally didn't do it either."

Her eyes widened. "If Sally didn't do it, then you think—"

I nodded. "I think Bonnie did it. It was the only way she was going to get her hands on the property."

"That's an awful lot of murder to get a piece of property."

"I think the property is worth quite a bit. Ty tried to, unsuccessfully, sell his parent's farm. Now he'll probably sell Esme's."

She nodded, completely unsurprised. "Ty was bragging about it this morning. I wanted to punch him. Everyone knows that house rightfully belongs to you."

"But he did so much for Esme. He deserves it way more than I do."

"He didn't do that much for Esme." She shifted her weight from one foot to another. "Sure, he worked the farm and kept the house in decent shape—at least inside

—but she paid him for that. Handsomely. It wasn't like he was doing it out of the kindness of his heart."

"But he made it sound like he was practically a grandson to her."

"If grandsons typically use their grandmothers for money, then sure." She shrugged. "You should fight it. Ty shouldn't get that house."

Fight it? How? I couldn't afford a stack of pancakes, let alone a lawyer. And I'd never ask Earl to take the case, especially when he didn't want to use his attorney license.

"I have to go," I said. "Thanks for the information. I'll see you tomorrow."

I jumped up into Mona's driver's seat and turned the key, but she wouldn't start.

"Come on, not today," I said. "I need to talk to someone about this case."

The ignition tried, but the engine didn't roar to life.

I sighed. "Mona, please. We need to do this. They have the wrong woman in jail. Please?" I laid my head on the steering wheel and turned the key one more time.

This time she sputtered to life. "Good girl. Thank you."

The cold must have been hard on her. I'd have to remember that as it got colder.

I drove back with my scalp feeling like sparks were flying off it.

I pulled a strand of my hair from my bun to confirm that it was orange bordering on red.

When I pulled into Helen's driveway, I wasn't the only one there. Ty's truck was parked out front right next to the Des Moines Developer truck PJ had been driving.

Bonnie opened the door, and my hair felt like it might explode into a fireball.

I'd only ever felt it this strongly once before. When I was a teenager. I hit a girl in the face with a volleyball in gym class, and she charged me with the anger of a bull. I mean, she hated me before then, but in that moment, she was mad enough to kill.

Bonnie didn't look like a killer in her tight jeans, ankle boots, and knit sweater, but my hair said otherwise.

"Can I help you?" she asked.

I froze. I hadn't considered what I'd say when she opened the door. I couldn't just come out and say I knew she killed all these people.

"Uh." I looked back at Mona and Ty's truck. "Is Ty here? I need to talk to him."

She frowned. "He's here. We were discussing some business."

I resisted the urge to reach up and touch my hair to

make sure it hadn't actually started on fire. Not that it would, but it felt like it was.

"I just needed to ask him a quick question."

"Ty," she said over her shoulder. "The neighbor girl is here."

Ty peeked from around the corner. "Ellie?"

"Hey, Ty," I said, still trying to figure out what I was going to do. "I just needed to talk to you about transferring the property. I think we have more to discuss."

Anger flashed over his face. "More to discuss? What more is there to discuss?"

He came to stand next to Bonnie.

"Um, well." I needed to come up with something. "I wanted to know if I could take a couple of items. You know, to remember my grandma by?"

"Remember her? You never knew her."

His words cut like a knife to my heart.

"I know," I said. "I just—"

"Let her take what she wants," Bonnie said. "The house is going to be torn down."

Ty seemed to consider this, then said, "Fine. But nothing of great value. I can sell that and increase my profit."

Bonnie nodded.

"Great," I said. But it wasn't great. I wasn't getting anywhere. "I also wanted to tell you I don't think Sally killed all those people."

Both of the faces in front of me turned angry.

"Are you saying I lied?" Ty asked.

I shrugged. "I think it was a traumatic experience. You may have thought it was Sally, but it was someone else."

"Who?" Ty said. "Who else could it have been?"

I didn't know what came over me, but I blurted out. "It was her." My arm raised, finger pointed, right at the woman standing in front of me. "The only way she could get the farm was to kill all those people. If any of them were still alive, she wouldn't be able to claim ownership." I stopped to take a breath. "She didn't kill you because she knew you were going to get Esme's farm. And I'm guessing that the property is more valuable when there is more land. Since our properties border one another, she needed you alive to claim Esme's property."

Ty's face was still angry. "That's ridiculous."

Bonnie nodded. "I didn't kill anyone. I was in Chicago until the night before last."

"Do you have any way to prove that?" I asked. I knew for a fact she'd been in town far longer than that, and it was her truck I'd seen at the café that first shift, not PJ's.

"My darling," Bonnie said. "You are not the police. I do not have to answer any of your questions."

"Don't worry, I'm sure the police will question you shortly," I said.

"Okay, that's enough," Ty said. "Let's get over to Esme's so you can show me what you want to keep." He looked at his watch. "You have less than an hour."

I'd wasted the entire morning tracking down Bonnie when I could have spent more time at Esme's house. But it would be worth it when the right woman was behind bars.

Ty followed me in his truck as I turned Mona into Esme's driveway one last time.

"It'll be okay," I said. "It's just a house. It's not like I'm losing a grandmother."

Mona didn't respond. Obviously, because she was a van.

Ty walked inside with me, and Penelope greeted us with a loud squeal. She hadn't expected Ty. "It's okay." I picked her up. "Let's go get our stuff."

"While you're at it, I'll pour us a drink," Ty said. "To commemorate the day."

I wasn't a drinker, but I didn't tell Ty that. It would keep him out of my hair just long enough to get Esme's journal and lock up the attic without his intruding eyes.

I hurried upstairs as quickly as I could without drawing suspicion.

Once in the attic, I slipped the small notebook under my shirt, closed the secret door, then grabbed Big Bertha and hauled her down the stairs.

Ty met me at the bottom with a glass of amber-colored liquid in fancy crystal glasses. Penelope oinked from the top of the stairs.

"Why isn't she coming down?" Ty asked.

"She doesn't like stairs," I said, walking back up and carrying her down. "Her legs don't work well coming down them."

Ty looked at us skeptically. I put Penelope on the ground, trying not to spill the drink I held in my hand.

"I think this moment requires a toast," Ty said, wrapping an arm around my shoulders. "To Esme. May we all strive to be as wonderful as she was."

He smelled like a mix of floral and mint. My mind felt like a Tetris piece fell perfectly into place.

I pulled away from Ty.

"What?" Ty said. "Aren't you going to take a drink?"

I glanced down at the glass. I knew at that moment, it was poisoned. I set the glass on the counter. "I'm not much of a drinker."

"That's too bad," Ty said, draining his glass. And that was why multiple bottles were open in the cupboard.

"You did it," I whispered. "You killed them. All of them."

29

Ty smiled. "You really should stop accusing people of murder. It's not a good look on you." He poured himself another glass. "If you had been paying attention, I have an alibi. I was watching my favorite TV show. It was on in the bedroom upstairs."

I thought back to the television show—the one with Melody in the starring role.

"What happened at the beginning of the show?" I asked.

"The same thing that happens at the beginning of every episode," he said, his voice almost too cocky. "She changes into her tiger outfit and does some pull-ups on the bridge."

Now I knew.

Hank had commented about Melody's spinning kick-flip—something she'd never done before. And Ty had no clue. Because at that moment, he was murdering his uncle.

"Don't tell Sally—not that it matters now that she's in

jail—but I always had a thing for Melody." He finished the whiskey in his glass. "I asked her to prom junior year, but she turned me down. She was always too good for everyone."

I didn't want to talk about Melody or who Ty asked to prom. "That night, you poisoned your aunt and uncle, but it didn't do the trick. Helen got sick and threw it all up. Percy knew what you'd done and confronted you."

"That didn't happen," Ty said. "Sally and I were at dinner. Aunt Helen got sick, so we left to watch the show."

"But no one else got sick?" I asked. "Not you or Sally? Only Helen and Percy?"

Ty shrugged.

"What happened then?" I asked. "Did Percy chase after you with a knife from his kitchen?"

Ty's face twisted. "If he had, and I killed him, it would have been self-defense."

"Except you tried to poison him first," I said. "And when the poison hit him, he became weak. You took the knife and stabbed him."

Ty turned away from me and looked out the window over the sink.

"And the next day, you came over with the combine complete with chopping head. You were going to run over his dead body, weren't you? If I hadn't found him, he would have been . . ." I couldn't finish the sentence. It was too much to take in.

"That's disgusting," he said. "You have a sick mind."

"But Helen was still alive, and then PJ showed up. You didn't know about PJ, did you?"

"No one knew about PJ."

"Helen did."

"She was an idiot staying with him. For not signing that prenup."

"So naturally, you had to kill both of them," I said. "But you had to make it look like PJ did it, right? You found Helen at her house after you and Sally fought. Sally wasn't there at all. And I doubt you'd try to protect her by saying PJ did it because you don't care about her."

Ty didn't reply.

"You stabbed Helen and blood got all over your shirt. Your brown and *blue* shirt. When PJ showed up after finishing his meal at Grazie, you held him at gunpoint and made him exchange shirts with you. That's why his brown and *green* shirt was in your personal belongings bag from the hospital."

Ty gripped the edge of the counter so tightly his knuckles were white.

"I thought it was strange that a shell casing and one bullet hole were under the small table by Helen's front door, but it was so obvious. How would a shell casing get all the way across the room if PJ shot at you from where he stabbed Helen? And where were the other bullet holes from all those shots he missed? And how did the one bullet hole in the floor seem to be shot from above?"

I knew I was right. It took all this time, but I knew I was right. I needed to call Jake.

"Say I did do this," Ty growled. "Not that I did. But no one will believe you."

"They will when I show them all the evidence. Did you know PJ was right-handed?"

"What does that matter?"

"You put the gun in his left hand. He was shot in the chest from the left. That's why the bullet missed his heart. But besides the fact that PJ hated guns, he would have never shot himself with his left hand."

"You think you're so smart," Ty said, turning toward me. "You never found out about me breaking into your place."

"Breaking into this house?" I glanced around. Then I remembered. "Penelope didn't soil the carpet. It was mud, wasn't it? From your boots."

Penelope oinked loudly, confirming my thought.

"The boots you were wearing when you came to the funeral. And you had been on the phone with Sally."

He smiled.

"But you didn't find what you were looking for," I said.

"How do you know that?"

I didn't know how I knew that, but I did. With one hundred percent certainty. "Was it the papers?"

"Sally tried to get them at the bank after you practically just dropped them in my lap," Ty said. "But she couldn't get her key to work. And when I broke in here, that stupid pig tried to attack me when I came into the bedroom. I had no choice but to lock him up."

"Her," I corrected. "Penelope is a girl."

At this point, my hair could have been a fireball for all I knew. It had warned me the night I'd met Ty, but I thought it was embarrassment. How could I have been so stupid?

"For what it's worth," I said. "I think it took a lot of nerve to shoot yourself in the leg. But you had to, so it looked like PJ did it. Were you planning on killing Bonnie next? I mean, at that point, surely you'd get the farm, right?"

"I may have tried to get the paperwork—which I didn't need because you were too stupid to read it and do what it said," he said. "But I didn't kill anyone. I take back what I said before. You can't have anything from this house. Get out."

I stood my ground. "This is my house. I'm not going anywhere."

"You had six months," Ty said. "You missed your window."

"Because you purposely sent the paperwork to the wrong address," I said. "I think the court will take that, plus the fact that you're a murderer, into account."

A knock at the door came from behind me, and with the slight diversion of attention from Ty, he lunged at me.

30

I only registered the knife as it went directly into my stomach. I fell to my knees, gripping the handle. I didn't know whether it was because my hair was already burning a hole through my skull or I was in shock, but the stab wound didn't hurt nearly as much as I expected it to.

The door flung open.

"What in the world?" Katie screamed. "What have you done?" She raced to my side while Earl rushed at Ty, tackling him to the ground.

I pulled my hand away from the knife, expecting to find blood, but it was clean.

"Don't take it out," Katie said. "It could be plugging a cut artery or something. We need to get you to the hospital."

I reached down to grab the knife again, but it fell on the floor in front of me with a small thud.

Katie picked it up and inspected it. "There's no blood on it."

It was at that moment I remembered I'd placed Esme's journal under my shirt.

Esme had saved my life.

I pulled the journal out to find a slice through the cover and pages about halfway through.

"You're one lucky little lady," Katie said.

"She's a witch," Ty yelled from underneath Earl. "Just like her stupid grandmother."

I stood and went over to him. "Don't you dare talk about my grandmother like that," I said. "She was anything but stupid."

Katie laughed.

Jake bounded through the door, Penelope right behind him. She must have gone out to lead him inside.

He took Earl's place and snapped handcuffs on Ty's wrists while I explained everything.

"And before you take him away," Earl said. "I just want him to know, Ellie owns the house. The moment she claimed residence, I—Esme's attorney—filed the paperwork on her behalf."

Tears sprung to my eyes, and my hair fire extinguished.

"Thank you so much," I said, hugging Earl. He stiffened at first, then returned the hug.

"It's truly my pleasure," he said. "Now, get him out of here."

Jake saluted Earl and loaded Ty into the patrol car's back seat where Sally had been mere hours before.

When Jake came back inside, I told him everything. From the whiskey to the knife to the ring—which was not Ty's, but Percy's from some secret farmer society. Earl was very tight-lipped about it when I brought it up.

"I'm impressed," Katie said when I'd finished. "I know Esme helped the police department now and again, but what you did tonight—what you came up with—was the work of a true detective."

"I'm just a therapeutic recreation specialist slash waitress," I said. "And some people think I'm a witch."

Katie and Earl laughed.

"How does it feel to be home, kiddo?" Earl asked.

"It feels more perfect than anything has ever felt in my life," I said. "Thank you for all of your help."

"Now, can I fill your closet with all of Melody's old clothes?" Katie asked, her hands folded in front of her as if she was begging.

"I suppose so," I said. "It's not like I'm going to be able to afford clothes with all the overdue bills I have."

"What overdue bills?" Earl asked. "Esme left plenty of money to keep the house going. She didn't want you to have any trouble living here." Then a look of recognition crossed his face. "Is that why you were putting food in your purse after Percy's funeral?"

I blushed. I'd hoped no one had seen that. "Where exactly is this money?"

"It's in the bank," Earl said. "Did you read any of the paperwork?"

"I tried," I said. "But it was so jargon-y."

"How about we go over all of it together?" Earl said. "I should have done that in the first place, but I needed to know that you'd fit in with the town. That you weren't just going to come in, sell Esme's place, take her money, and leave."

"Why would I do that?" I asked.

"You may have a lot of your grandmother in you," Katie said gently. "But you also have some of your mother. And your mother was a runner."

I'd been a runner my entire life. But now, I wouldn't run. Now, I would stay.

This was my home.

"We should leave Ellie alone," Katie said to Earl.

"Will I see you at the café tomorrow?" Earl asked.

"Absolutely," I said. "Until my business takes off, I think I'll keep waitressing."

"Bex and I are both so happy to have you on the team," Katie said. "Get some sleep."

We said our goodbyes, and Penelope and I made our way upstairs. When I snuggled into Esme's bed—my bed—I felt like a boulder had been lifted off my shoulders.

I leaned over the side and scratched Penelope behind the ear. "It feels good to be home, doesn't it?"

She let out a tired little oink in agreement.

The next morning at the café, everyone had already heard about what happened. Bex hugged me about fifteen times within the first hour. Hank didn't come for coffee.

By the end of my shift, I was ready to go home and enjoy the feeling of not being in the middle of an investigation. Not be worried about a murderer on the loose. And to see the mural in the barn again.

I pulled Mona into the garage, shut her off, and made my way to the barn. With a great deal of effort and some encouragement in the form of piggy squeals, I slid both of the big barn doors open on their rusty tracks letting in a flood of bright sunlight.

Dust floated in the air like tiny little fairy lights that made Penelope sneeze.

I made my way around an old tractor and a bunch of random tools. How I'd gotten through all of this in the dark was beyond me.

When I reached the back of the barn, I couldn't believe

what my eyes were seeing. Or rather, not seeing. The mural of the farm was still there, but the women I'd seen in the light of my phone flashlight were gone.

"What happened to them?" I asked Penelope who just gave me a confused look.

A silly idea popped into my head. I pulled my phone from my satchel and turned on the flashlight.

Even though the light was completely unnecessary, I shined it on the mural where the women had been. Nothing.

I turned it off and put it back in my satchel.

"Ellie?" Jake's voice came from the front of the barn. "Are you in here?"

"Back here," I said, not turning around.

Jake came to stand next to me. "She really was something."

I glanced over at him.

"I may have lied before when I said we were just acquaintances."

"I know." I turned back to the mural. "Sally told me."

"I figured you'd find out." Jake was quiet for a minute. "I know what you're probably thinking."

I stayed silent. Sometimes letting someone talk without interruption resulted in more information.

"I'm not your father, Ellie," he said. "As much as I wish it were the case."

"If it's not you, then who?"

He sighed. "Trust me. I've been asking myself that same question since the moment Esme told me about you. She told me first, you know?"

"Because she thought . . ." I couldn't finish the

sentence. Disappointment flowed through my veins. I didn't realize how much I wanted Jake to be my father until I found out he wasn't.

"But when I told her it wasn't possible, she was just as disappointed as I am right now. As I have been since I found out."

"What about our eyes?" I was grasping at any hope I could, which would only lead to more disappointment. But maybe he'd forgotten something. Maybe he'd blocked out that one time he and Emily . . . you know.

"It's strange, isn't it?" Jake asked. "That was the first thing I noticed about you. How in the world do we have the same eyes? I've asked myself the same thing. But honestly, if it wasn't the eyes, it would have been something else. We would have had the same hands or the same toes or the same hair." He looked at my hair, which was probably about fifteen shades of crazy right now. "Okay, maybe not the same hair." He let out a little laugh. "I wish I would have handled it better," he said. "When we first met. I didn't mean to be so dismissive. I just didn't know what to do."

"What happened with Emily? Why did she leave?"

"Some people will try to convince you that Emily was flighty, or trouble, or dangerous, even. But she was none of those things," he said. "I don't know the reason, but she must have had good reason to leave. She loved Esme. They didn't have the typical mother-daughter relationship full of bickering and drama—at least that's how my mom and sisters were. Esme and Emily were best friends. When Emily left, Esme's heart broke. She was never the same until she found out about you."

He reached an arm out and squeezed my shoulder.

"You brought hope back into her eyes. Love back into her heart."

Tears trickled down my cheeks. "Do you think Emily's dead?"

When Jake didn't answer, I glanced up to find tears on his cheeks as well.

"I sincerely hope she isn't," he said. "There's not a day that goes by that I don't think about her."

"I take it you haven't gotten married?"

He shook his head. "Couldn't. Every woman I dated could never compare to my first love. Some women have accused Emily of putting a love spell on me. But it's not like that. Emily was so many things wrapped up in a tiny little package. Fire and ice, power and beauty." He looked down at me. "All the same things I see in you."

Why couldn't he be my father? Why had Emily had a baby with someone else? I wanted to ask Jake but didn't want to bring him any more pain.

"I'm sorry she left," I said, knowing that if more than twenty years hadn't healed his heart, my words wouldn't either.

"As I said, she must have had a good reason." He wiped the tears from his cheeks. "I just hope someday I'll know what that reason was."

One more thing we had in common.

Thank you so much for reading *Downward Death*!

· · ·

The second book in the Magical Mane Mystery series —*Bowling Blunder*—releases March 16, 2021.

And if you haven't read it yet, check out the Rylie Cooper Mystery series, a humorous mystery series similar to Janet Evanovich's Stephanie Plum novels.

I would be honored and eternally grateful if you would post a review on Amazon and/or Goodreads about the book.

Also, I love hearing from readers! Email me at stellabixbyauthor@gmail.com.

XOXO,

Stella Bixby

ACKNOWLEDGMENTS

I'd like to thank Iowa first. I know, it's weird to thank an entire state. Do I mean the people? The land? The towns? Yes to all of the above! I never thought I'd love any state other than Colorado, then I moved to Iowa and my mind slowly changed. It has been a great pleasure writing a book in such a wonderful, yet underrated, state.

God, Family, and Friends are the pillars of my life. Without them, I would be nothing. There would be no writing. No books. No me.

Nolan, you're my rock and my biggest supporter. Thank you a million times over. My heart gravitates toward you.

Faith and Lily, I couldn't have done this without your support and help with the boys. Thank you so much. I'm thankful every day that I'm your mom.

Grant and Christian, you've opened my eyes to the beauty of chaos. Even when it drives me crazy. I love you both.

Thank you to my beta readers. You will never know how much I appreciate you. I couldn't make these books without your help!

And to my new and loyal fans, you're the reason I write. I hope I can bring even the slightest bit of joy to your life. Thank you for reading my books.

ABOUT THE AUTHOR

Stella Bixby is a native Coloradan who loves to snow-board, pluck at the guitar, and play board games with her family. She was once a volunteer firefighter and a park ranger, but now spends most of her time making up stories and trying to figure out what to cook for dinner.

Connect with Stella on Facebook, Twitter, and Instagram @StellaBixby.

Stella loves to hear from her readers!
www.stellabixby.com

www.ingramcontent.com/pod-product-compliance
Lightning Source LLC
Chambersburg PA
CBHW021136190726
48288CB00008B/2688